# SYBIL
### the Backpack Fairy

## 4
## "Princess Nina"

MICHEL RODRIGUE • Writer
ANTONELLO DALENA & MANUELA RAZZI • Artists
CECILIA GIUMENTO • Colorist

WITHDRAWN

## PAPERCUTZ
New York

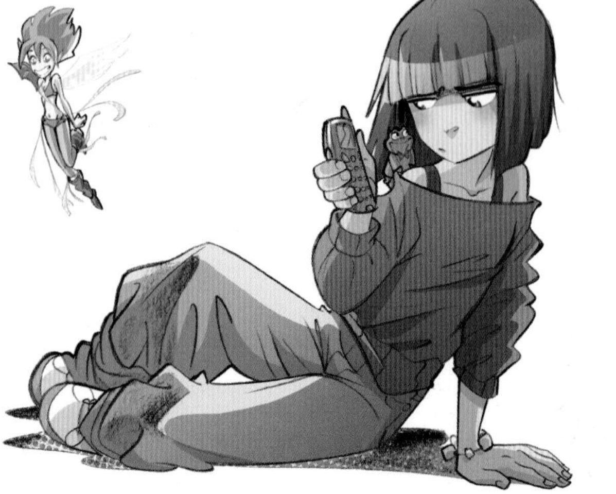

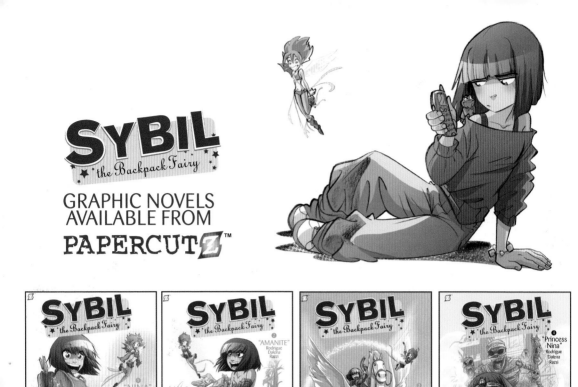

# SYBIL the Backpack Fairy

## GRAPHIC NOVELS AVAILABLE FROM PAPERCUTZ™

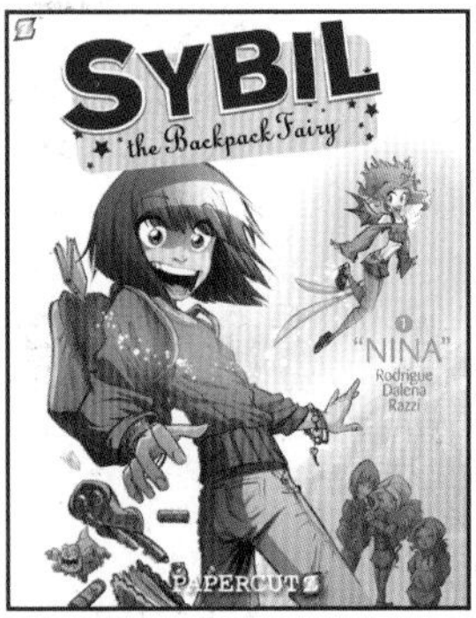

SYBIL
the Backpack Fairy
1 "NINA"
Rodrigue
Dalena
Razzi
PAPERCUTZ


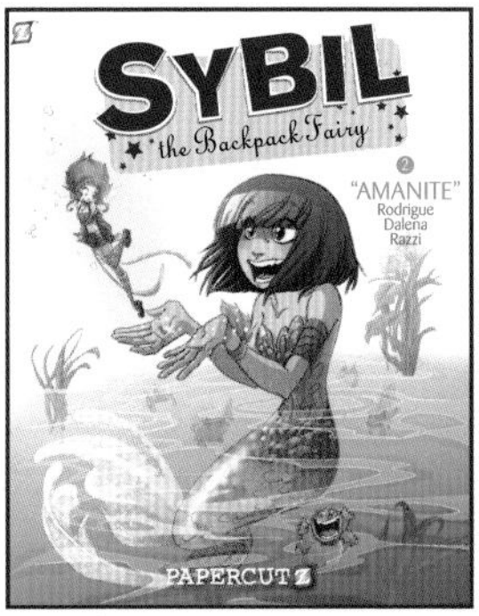

SYBIL
the Backpack Fairy
2 "AMANITE"
Rodrigue
Dalena
Razzi
PAPERCUTZ


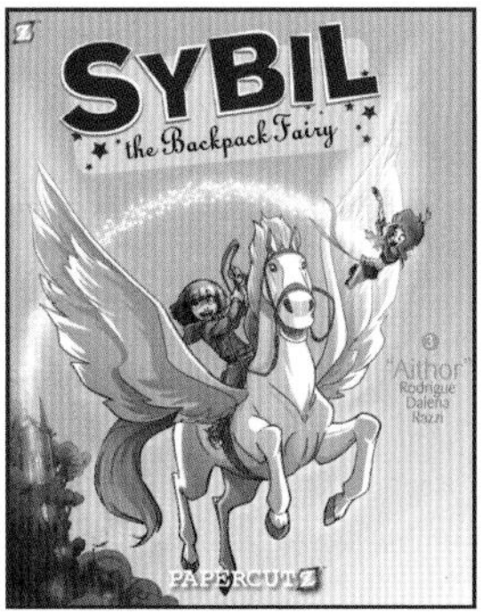

SYBIL
the Backpack Fairy
3 "Aithor"
Rodrigue
Dalena
Razzi
PAPERCUTZ


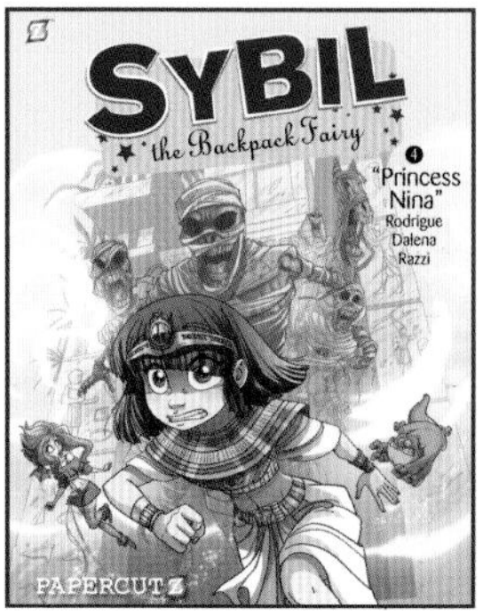

SYBIL
the Backpack Fairy
4 "Princess Nina"
Rodrigue
Dalena
Razzi
PAPERCUTZ


1 "NINA" 2 "AMANITE" 3 "AITHOR" 4 "PRINCESS NINA"

SYBIL THE BACKPACK FAIRY graphic novels are available in hardcover for $10.99 each, except #2, for $11.99 from booksellers everywhere. Order online at papercutz.com. Order by mail: please add $4.00 for postage and handling for first book ordered, and add $1.00 for each additional book. Please make check payable to NBM Publishing. Send to: Papercutz, 160 Broadway, Suite 700, East Wing, New York, NY 10038 or call 800 866 1223 (9-6 EST M-F) MC, Visa, AmEx accepted.


Sybil the Backpack Fairy
#4 "Princess Nina"
MICHEL RODRIGUE -- Writer
ANTONELLO DALENA & MANUELA RAZZI – Artists
CECILIA GIUMENTO -- Colorist
JOE JOHNSON -- Translation
TOM ORZECHOWSKI -- Lettering
BETH SCORZATO -- Production Coordinator
MICHAEL PETRANEK -- Editor
JIM SALICRUP
Editor-in-Chief




ISBN: 978-1-59707-415-5

Printed in China
June 2013 by New Era Printing, LTD
Unit C, 8/F, Worldwide Centre, 123 Tung Chau St
Kowloon, Hong Kong

Papercutz books maye be purchased for business or promtional use.
For information on bulk purchases please contact Macmillan Corporate and Premium Sales Department at (800) 221-7945 x5442

Distributed by Macmillan
First Papercutz Printing

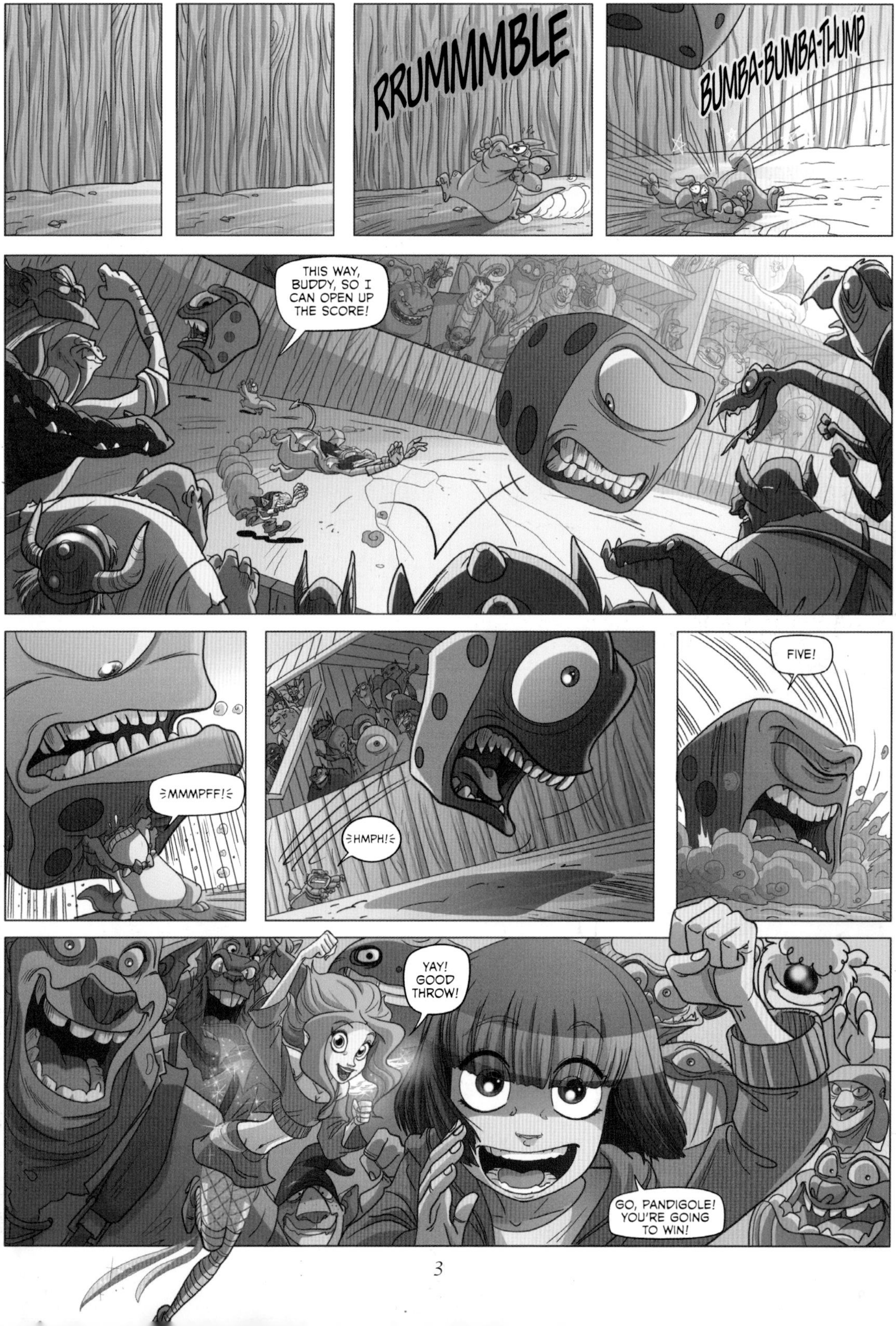

RRUMMMBLE
BUMBA-BUMBA-THUMP
THIS WAY, BUDDY, SO I CAN OPEN UP THE SCORE!
MMMPFF!
HMPH!
FIVE!
YAY! GOOD THROW!
GO, PANDIGOLE! YOU'RE GOING TO WIN!

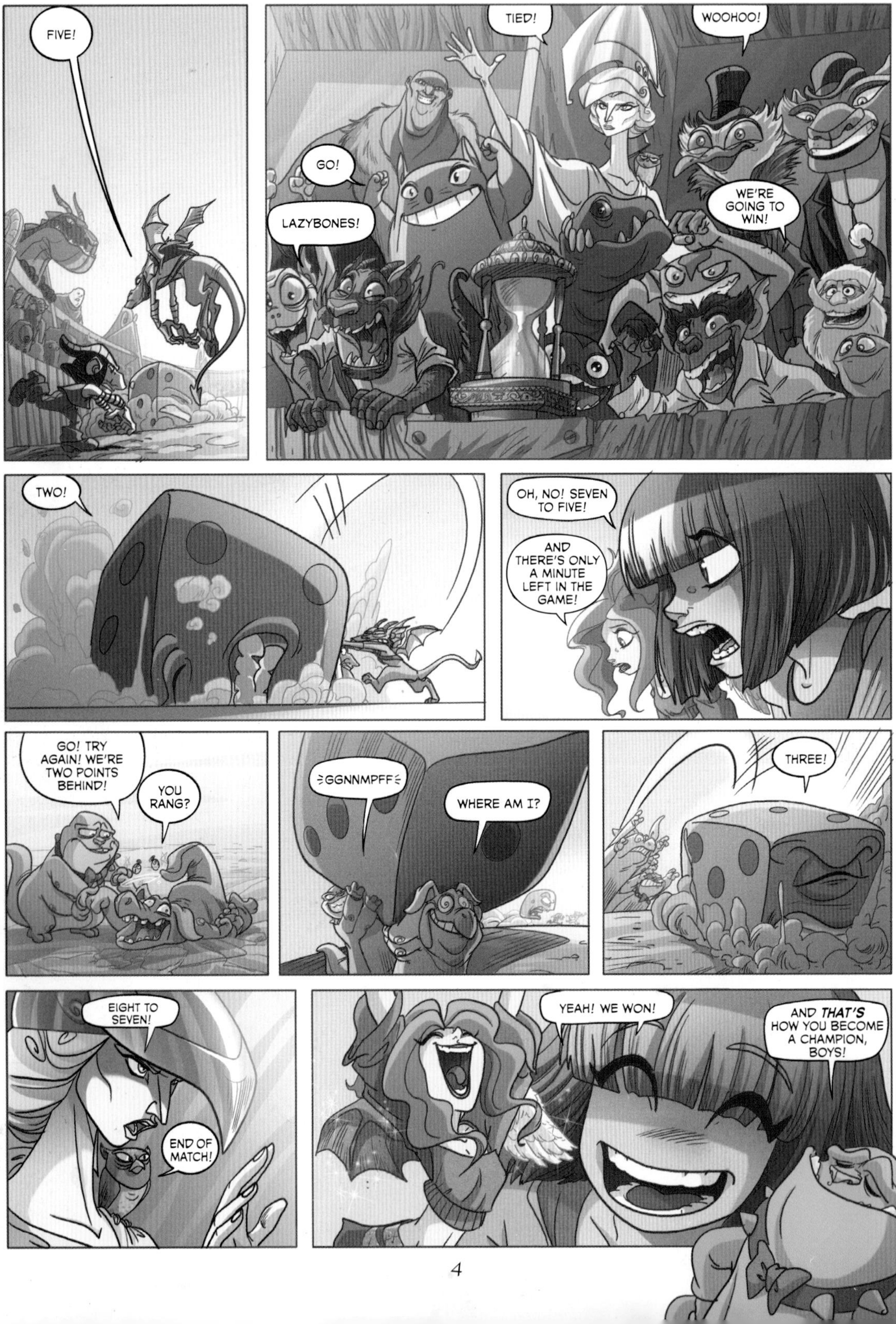
FIVE!
TIED!
WOOHOO!
GO!
LAZYBONES!
WE'RE GOING TO WIN!
TWO!
OH, NO! SEVEN TO FIVE!
AND THERE'S ONLY A MINUTE LEFT IN THE GAME!
GO! TRY AGAIN! WE'RE TWO POINTS BEHIND!
YOU RANG?
GGNNMPFF
WHERE AM I?
THREE!
EIGHT TO SEVEN!
END OF MATCH!
YEAH! WE WON!
AND *THAT'S* HOW YOU BECOME A CHAMPION, BOYS!

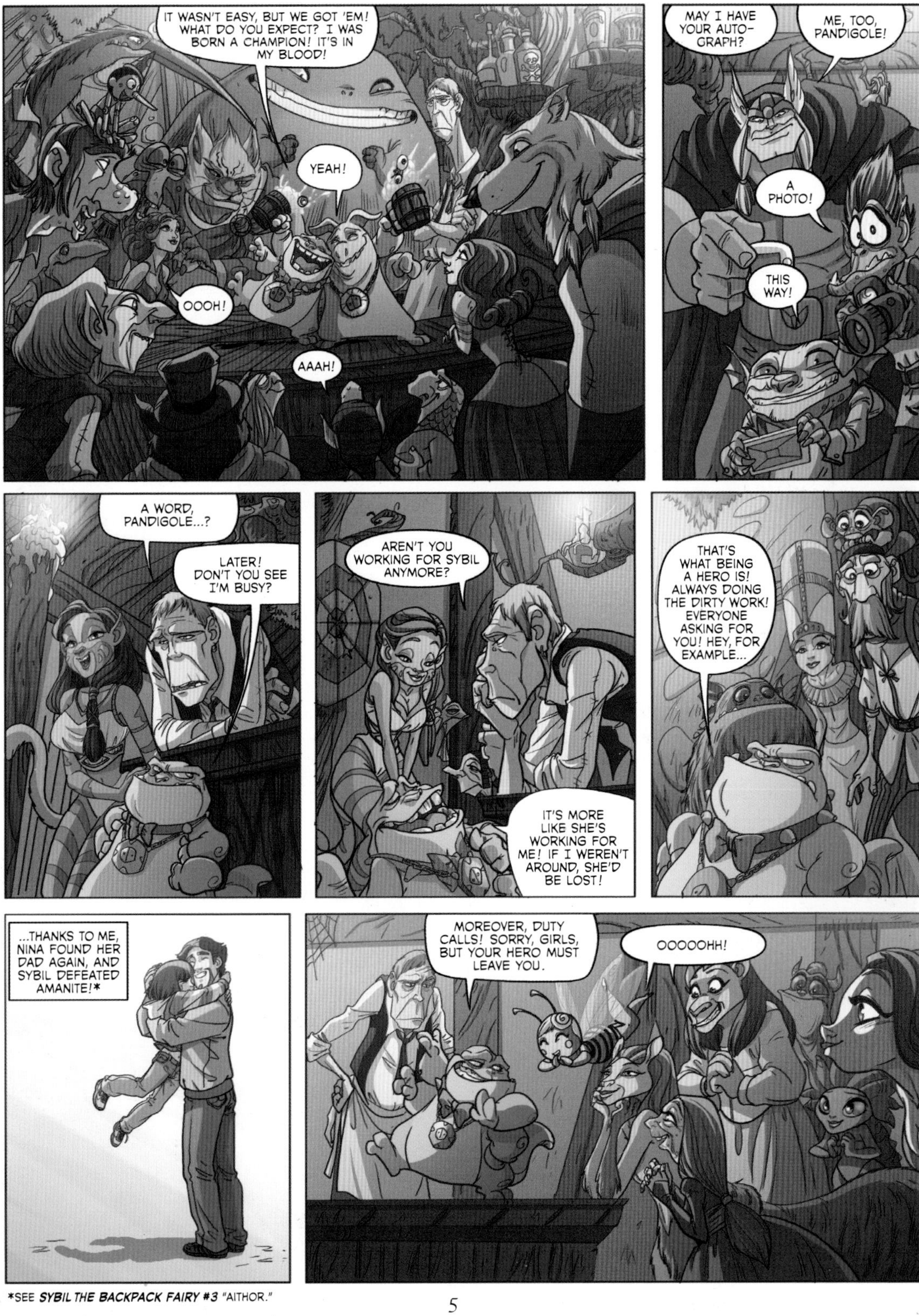
IT WASN'T EASY, BUT WE GOT 'EM! WHAT DO YOU EXPECT? I WAS BORN A CHAMPION! IT'S IN MY BLOOD!
YEAH!
OOOH!
AAAH!
MAY I HAVE YOUR AUTO-GRAPH?
ME, TOO, PANDIGOLE!
A PHOTO!
THIS WAY!
A WORD, PANDIGOLE...?
LATER! DON'T YOU SEE I'M BUSY?
AREN'T YOU WORKING FOR SYBIL ANYMORE?
IT'S MORE LIKE SHE'S WORKING FOR ME! IF I WEREN'T AROUND, SHE'D BE LOST!
THAT'S WHAT BEING A HERO IS! ALWAYS DOING THE DIRTY WORK! EVERYONE ASKING FOR YOU! HEY, FOR EXAMPLE...
...THANKS TO ME, NINA FOUND HER DAD AGAIN, AND SYBIL DEFEATED AMANITE!*
MOREOVER, DUTY CALLS! SORRY, GIRLS, BUT YOUR HERO MUST LEAVE YOU.
OOOOOHH!

*SEE ***SYBIL THE BACKPACK FAIRY #3*** "AITHOR."

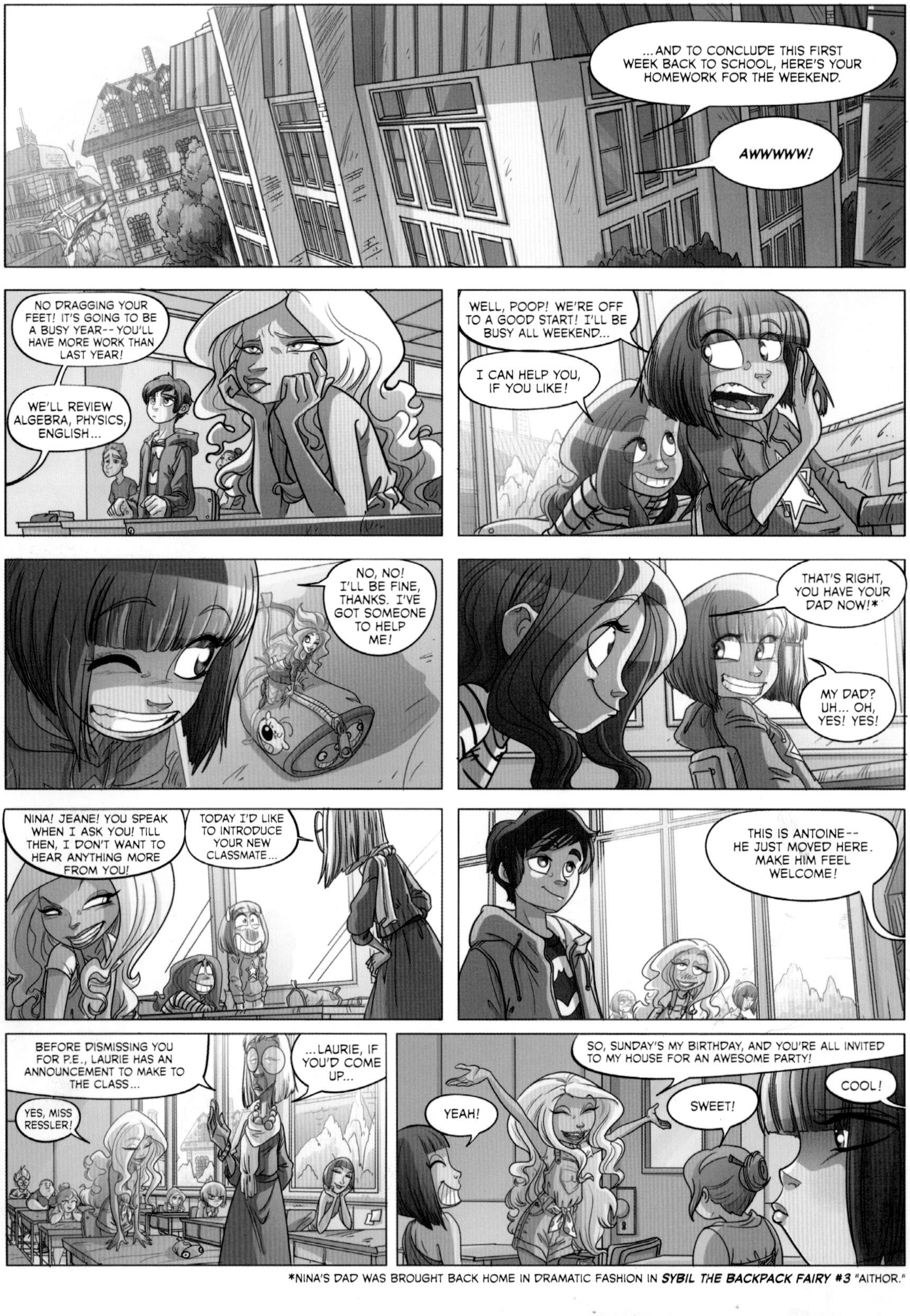
...AND TO CONCLUDE THIS FIRST WEEK BACK TO SCHOOL, HERE'S YOUR HOMEWORK FOR THE WEEKEND.
AWWWWW!
NO DRAGGING YOUR FEET! IT'S GOING TO BE A BUSY YEAR-- YOU'LL HAVE MORE WORK THAN LAST YEAR!
WE'LL REVIEW ALGEBRA, PHYSICS, ENGLISH...
WELL, POOP! WE'RE OFF TO A GOOD START! I'LL BE BUSY ALL WEEKEND...
I CAN HELP YOU, IF YOU LIKE!
NO, NO! I'LL BE FINE, THANKS. I'VE GOT SOMEONE TO HELP ME!
THAT'S RIGHT, YOU HAVE YOUR DAD NOW!*
MY DAD? UH... OH, YES! YES!
NINA! JEANE! YOU SPEAK WHEN I ASK YOU! TILL THEN, I DON'T WANT TO HEAR ANYTHING MORE FROM YOU!
TODAY I'D LIKE TO INTRODUCE YOUR NEW CLASSMATE...
THIS IS ANTOINE-- HE JUST MOVED HERE. MAKE HIM FEEL WELCOME!
BEFORE DISMISSING YOU FOR P.E., LAURIE HAS AN ANNOUNCEMENT TO MAKE TO THE CLASS...
...LAURIE, IF YOU'D COME UP...
YES, MISS RESSLER!
SO, SUNDAY'S MY BIRTHDAY, AND YOU'RE ALL INVITED TO MY HOUSE FOR AN AWESOME PARTY!
YEAH!
SWEET!
COOL!

*NINA'S DAD WAS BROUGHT BACK HOME IN DRAMATIC FASHION IN ***SYBIL THE BACKPACK FAIRY #3*** "AITHOR."

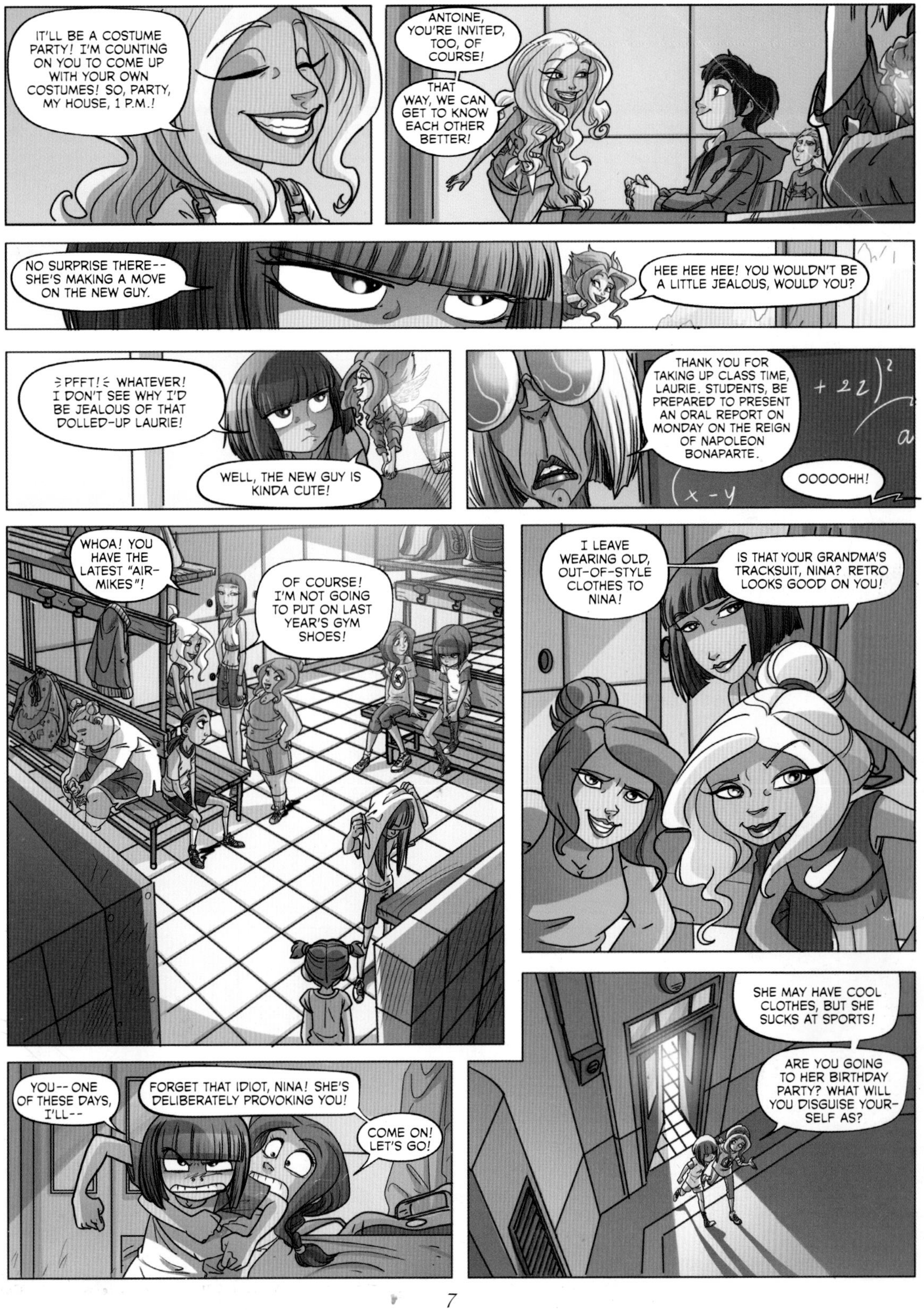
IT'LL BE A COSTUME PARTY! I'M COUNTING ON YOU TO COME UP WITH YOUR OWN COSTUMES! SO, PARTY, MY HOUSE, 1 P.M.!
ANTOINE, YOU'RE INVITED, TOO, OF COURSE!
THAT WAY, WE CAN GET TO KNOW EACH OTHER BETTER!
NO SURPRISE THERE-- SHE'S MAKING A MOVE ON THE NEW GUY.
HEE HEE HEE! YOU WOULDN'T BE A LITTLE JEALOUS, WOULD YOU?
≥PFFT!≤ WHATEVER! I DON'T SEE WHY I'D BE JEALOUS OF THAT DOLLED-UP LAURIE!
WELL, THE NEW GUY IS KINDA CUTE!
THANK YOU FOR TAKING UP CLASS TIME, LAURIE. STUDENTS, BE PREPARED TO PRESENT AN ORAL REPORT ON MONDAY ON THE REIGN OF NAPOLEON BONAPARTE.
OOOOOHH!
WHOA! YOU HAVE THE LATEST "AIR-MIKES"!
OF COURSE! I'M NOT GOING TO PUT ON LAST YEAR'S GYM SHOES!
I LEAVE WEARING OLD, OUT-OF-STYLE CLOTHES TO NINA!
IS THAT YOUR GRANDMA'S TRACKSUIT, NINA? RETRO LOOKS GOOD ON YOU!
YOU-- ONE OF THESE DAYS, I'LL--
FORGET THAT IDIOT, NINA! SHE'S DELIBERATELY PROVOKING YOU!
COME ON! LET'S GO!
SHE MAY HAVE COOL CLOTHES, BUT SHE SUCKS AT SPORTS!
ARE YOU GOING TO HER BIRTHDAY PARTY? WHAT WILL YOU DISGUISE YOUR-SELF AS?

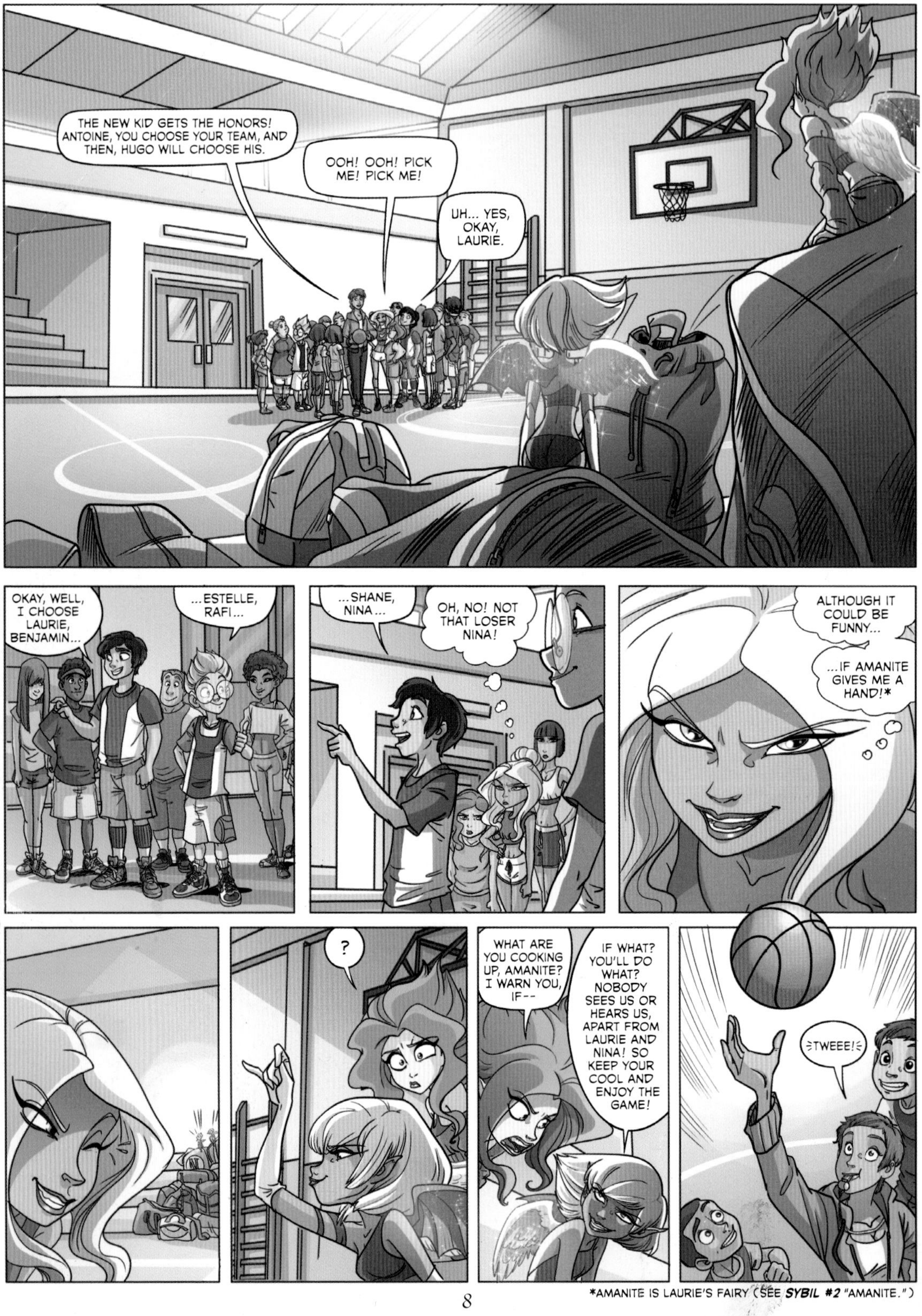
THE NEW KID GETS THE HONORS! ANTOINE, YOU CHOOSE YOUR TEAM, AND THEN, HUGO WILL CHOOSE HIS.
OOH! OOH! PICK ME! PICK ME!
UH... YES, OKAY, LAURIE.
OKAY, WELL, I CHOOSE LAURIE, BENJAMIN...
...ESTELLE, RAFI...
...SHANE, NINA...
OH, NO! NOT THAT LOSER NINA!
ALTHOUGH IT COULD BE FUNNY...
...IF AMANITE GIVES ME A HAND!*
?
WHAT ARE YOU COOKING UP, AMANITE? I WARN YOU, IF--
IF WHAT? YOU'LL DO WHAT? NOBODY SEES US OR HEARS US, APART FROM LAURIE AND NINA! SO KEEP YOUR COOL AND ENJOY THE GAME!
TWEEE!

*AMANITE IS LAURIE'S FAIRY (SEE ***SYBIL #2*** "AMANITE.")

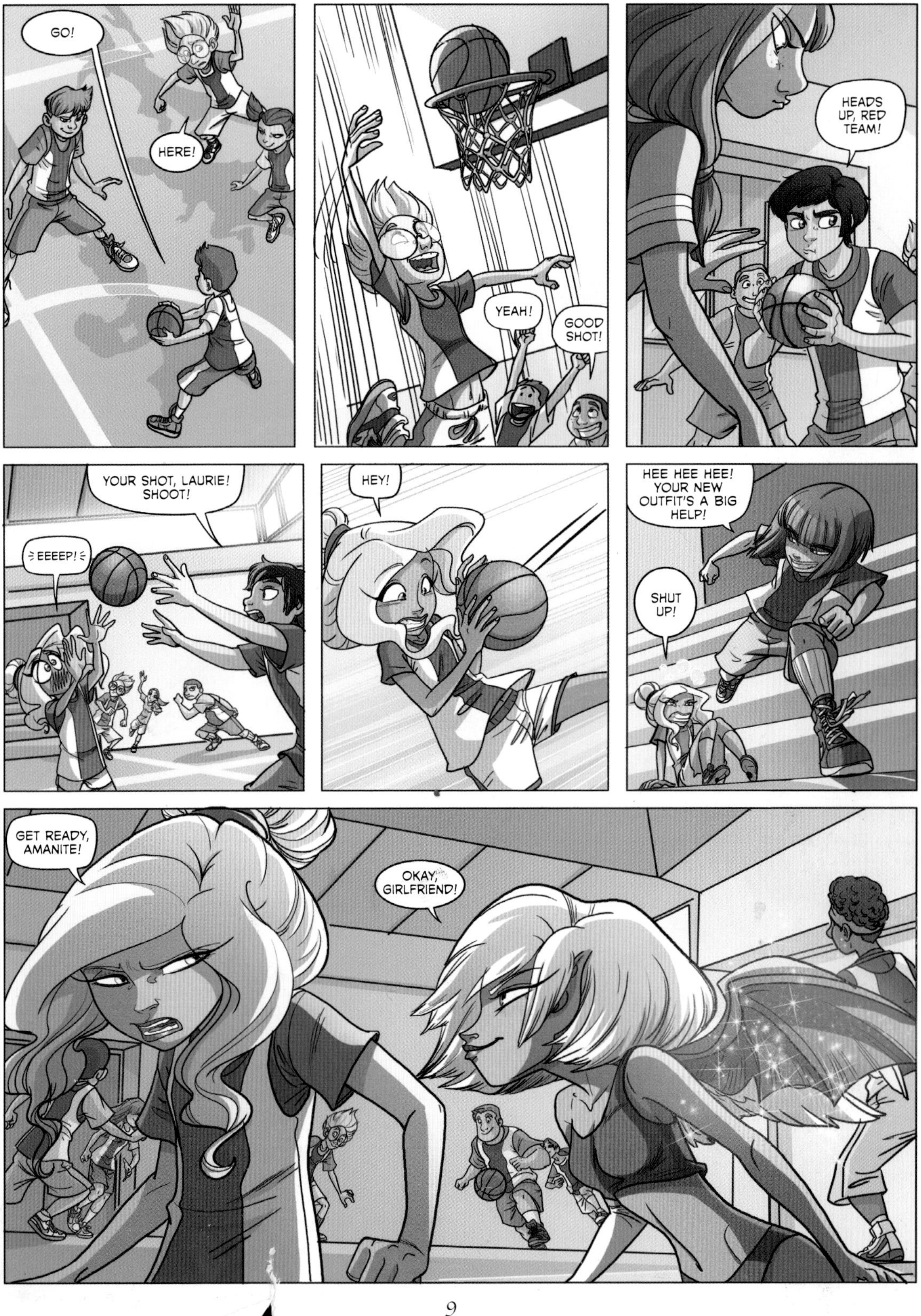
GO!
HERE!
YEAH!
GOOD SHOT!
HEADS UP, RED TEAM!
YOUR SHOT, LAURIE! SHOOT!
EEEEP!
HEY!
HEE HEE HEE! YOUR NEW OUTFIT'S A BIG HELP!
SHUT UP!
GET READY, AMANITE!
OKAY, GIRLFRIEND!

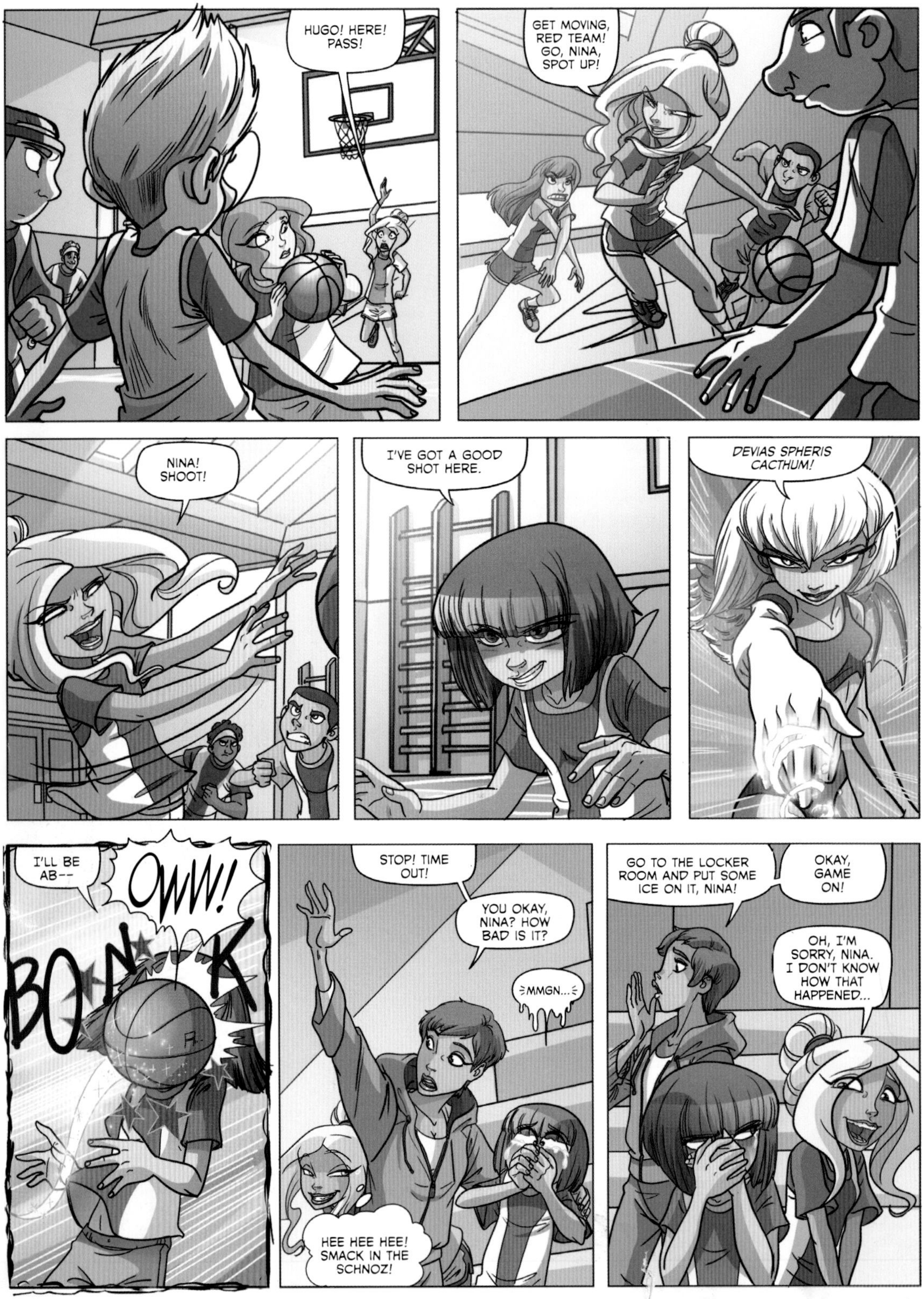
HUGO! HERE! PASS!
GET MOVING, RED TEAM! GO, NINA, SPOT UP!
NINA! SHOOT!
I'VE GOT A GOOD SHOT HERE.
*DEVIAS SPHERIS CACTHUM!*
I'LL BE AB--
OWW!
BONK
STOP! TIME OUT!
YOU OKAY, NINA? HOW BAD IS IT?
MMGN...
HEE HEE HEE! SMACK IN THE SCHNOZ!
GO TO THE LOCKER ROOM AND PUT SOME ICE ON IT, NINA!
OKAY, GAME ON!
OH, I'M SORRY, NINA. I DON'T KNOW HOW THAT HAPPENED...

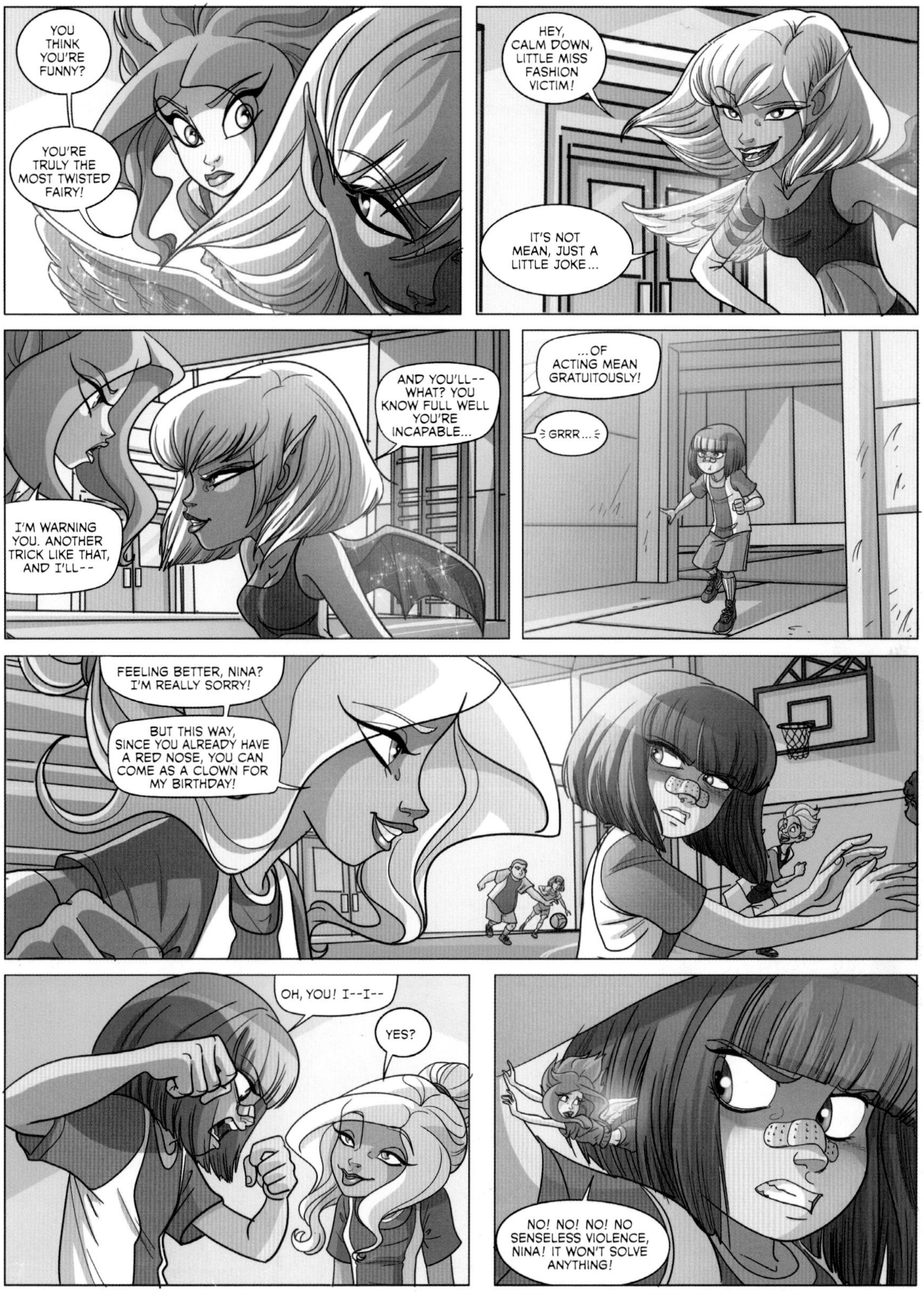
YOU THINK YOU'RE FUNNY?
YOU'RE TRULY THE MOST TWISTED FAIRY!
HEY, CALM DOWN, LITTLE MISS FASHION VICTIM!
IT'S NOT MEAN, JUST A LITTLE JOKE...
I'M WARNING YOU. ANOTHER TRICK LIKE THAT, AND I'LL--
AND YOU'LL-- WHAT? YOU KNOW FULL WELL YOU'RE INCAPABLE...
...OF ACTING MEAN GRATUITOUSLY!
GRRR...
FEELING BETTER, NINA? I'M REALLY SORRY!
BUT THIS WAY, SINCE YOU ALREADY HAVE A RED NOSE, YOU CAN COME AS A CLOWN FOR MY BIRTHDAY!
OH, YOU! I--I--
YES?
NO! NO! NO! NO SENSELESS VIOLENCE, NINA! IT WON'T SOLVE ANYTHING!

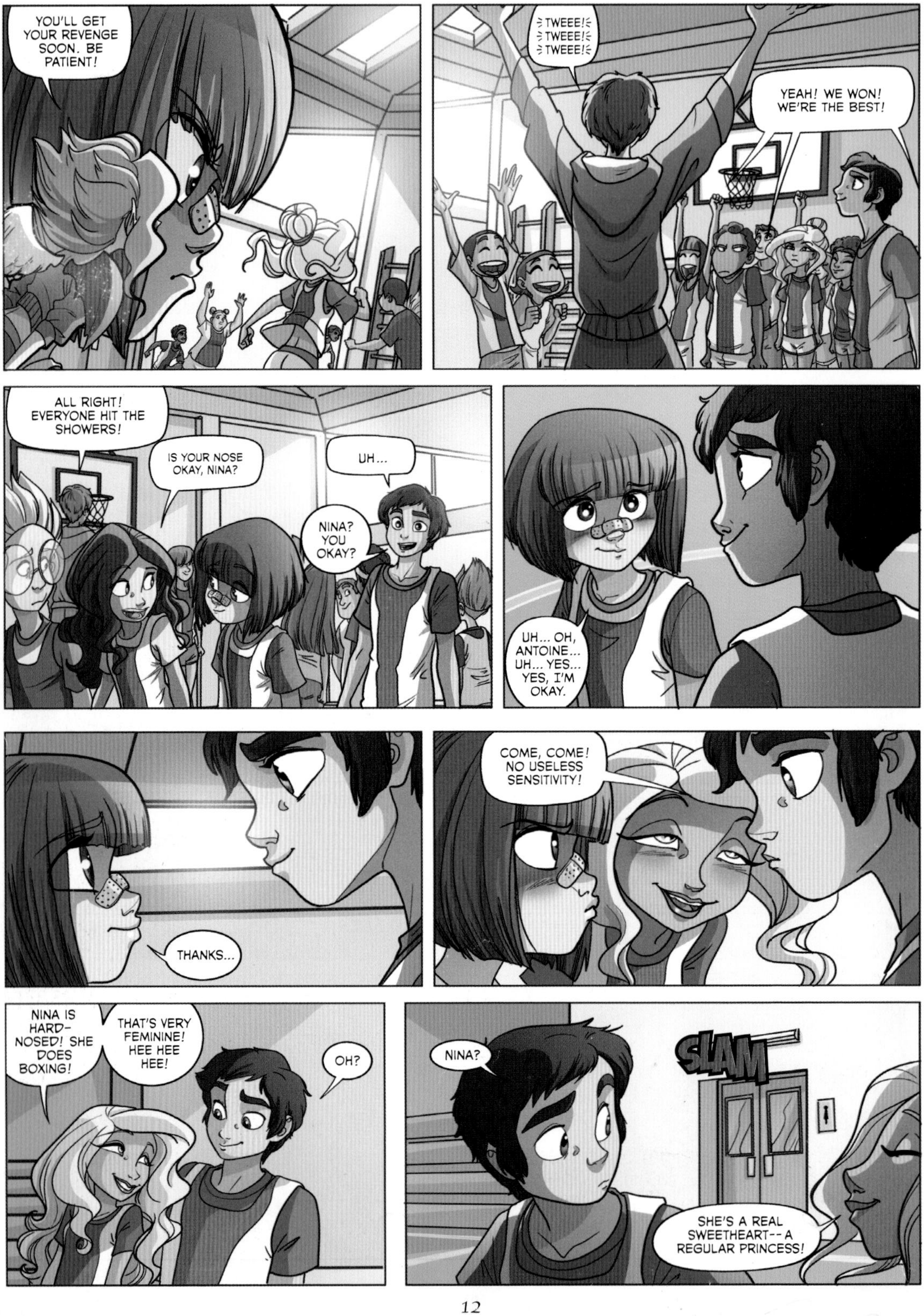
YOU'LL GET YOUR REVENGE SOON. BE PATIENT!
TWEEE! TWEEE! TWEEE!
YEAH! WE WON! WE'RE THE BEST!
ALL RIGHT! EVERYONE HIT THE SHOWERS!
IS YOUR NOSE OKAY, NINA?
UH...
NINA? YOU OKAY?
UH... OH, ANTOINE... UH... YES... YES, I'M OKAY.
THANKS...
COME, COME! NO USELESS SENSITIVITY!
NINA IS HARD-NOSED! SHE DOES BOXING!
THAT'S VERY FEMININE! HEE HEE HEE!
OH?
NINA?
SLAM
SHE'S A REAL SWEETHEART-- A REGULAR PRINCESS!

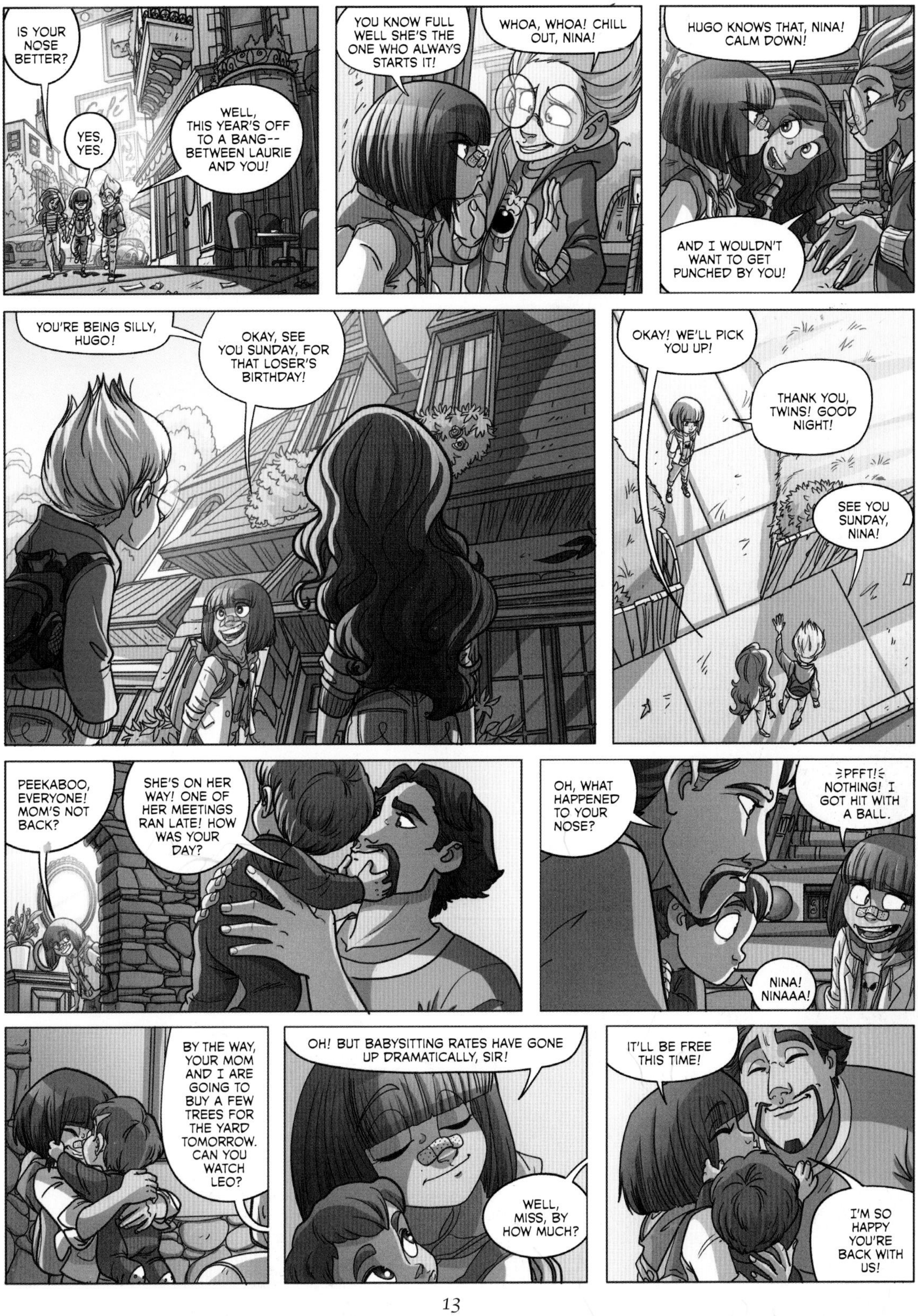
IS YOUR NOSE BETTER?
YES, YES.
WELL, THIS YEAR'S OFF TO A BANG-- BETWEEN LAURIE AND YOU!
YOU KNOW FULL WELL SHE'S THE ONE WHO ALWAYS STARTS IT!
WHOA, WHOA! CHILL OUT, NINA!
HUGO KNOWS THAT, NINA! CALM DOWN!
AND I WOULDN'T WANT TO GET PUNCHED BY YOU!
YOU'RE BEING SILLY, HUGO!
OKAY, SEE YOU SUNDAY, FOR THAT LOSER'S BIRTHDAY!
OKAY! WE'LL PICK YOU UP!
THANK YOU, TWINS! GOOD NIGHT!
SEE YOU SUNDAY, NINA!
PEEKABOO, EVERYONE! MOM'S NOT BACK?
SHE'S ON HER WAY! ONE OF HER MEETINGS RAN LATE! HOW WAS YOUR DAY?
OH, WHAT HAPPENED TO YOUR NOSE?
PFFT! NOTHING! I GOT HIT WITH A BALL.
NINA! NINAAA!
BY THE WAY, YOUR MOM AND I ARE GOING TO BUY A FEW TREES FOR THE YARD TOMORROW. CAN YOU WATCH LEO?
OH! BUT BABYSITTING RATES HAVE GONE UP DRAMATICALLY, SIR!
WELL, MISS, BY HOW MUCH?
IT'LL BE FREE THIS TIME!
I'M SO HAPPY YOU'RE BACK WITH US!

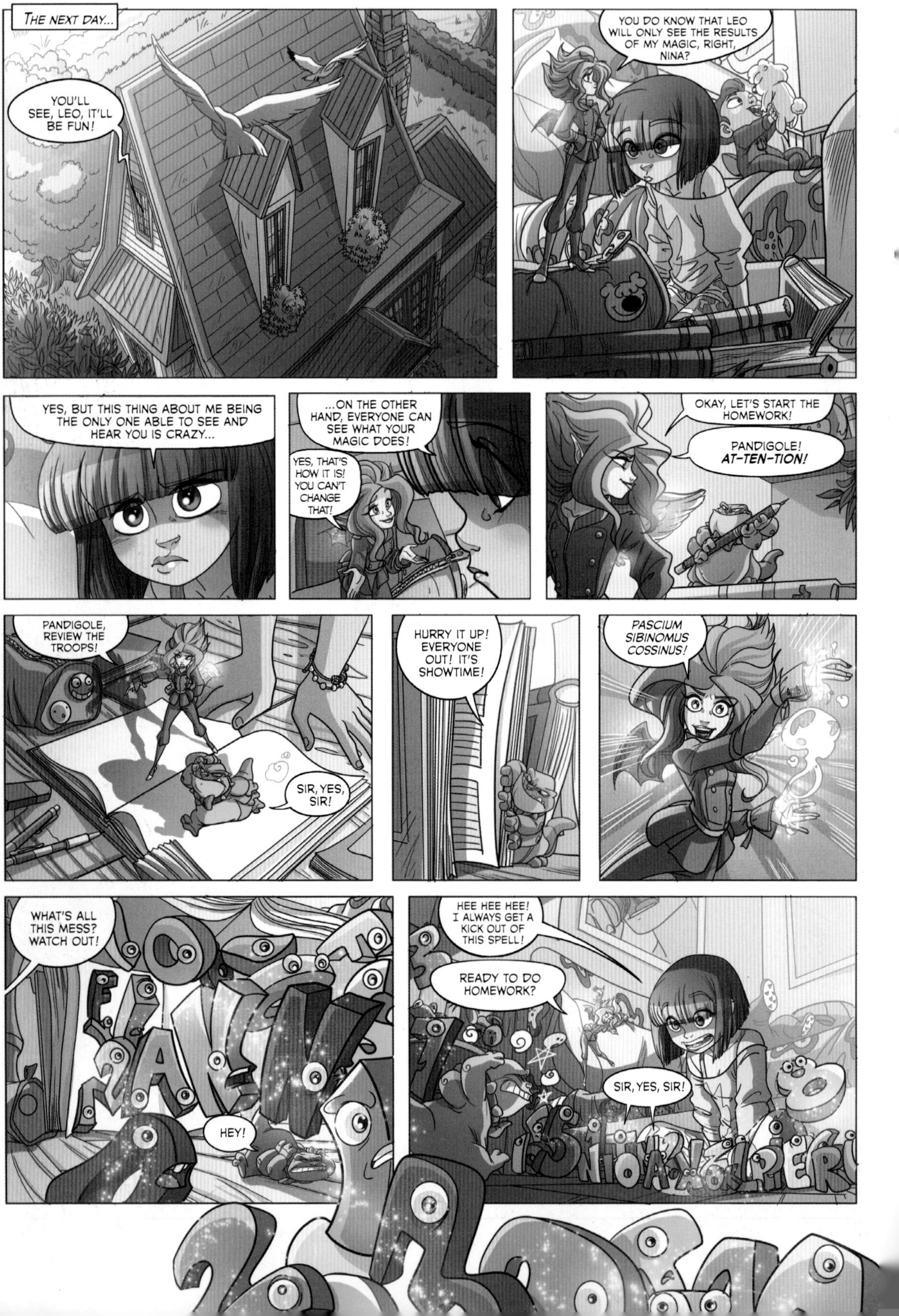
THE NEXT DAY...
YOU'LL SEE, LEO, IT'LL BE FUN!
YOU DO KNOW THAT LEO WILL ONLY SEE THE RESULTS OF MY MAGIC, RIGHT, NINA?
YES, BUT THIS THING ABOUT ME BEING THE ONLY ONE ABLE TO SEE AND HEAR YOU IS CRAZY...
...ON THE OTHER HAND, EVERYONE CAN SEE WHAT YOUR MAGIC DOES!
YES, THAT'S HOW IT IS! YOU CAN'T CHANGE THAT!
OKAY, LET'S START THE HOMEWORK!
PANDIGOLE! AT-TEN-TION!
PANDIGOLE, REVIEW THE TROOPS!
SIR, YES, SIR!
HURRY IT UP! EVERYONE OUT! IT'S SHOWTIME!
PASCIUM SIBINOMUS COSSINUS!
WHAT'S ALL THIS MESS? WATCH OUT!
HEY!
HEE HEE HEE! I ALWAYS GET A KICK OUT OF THIS SPELL!
READY TO DO HOMEWORK?
SIR, YES, SIR!

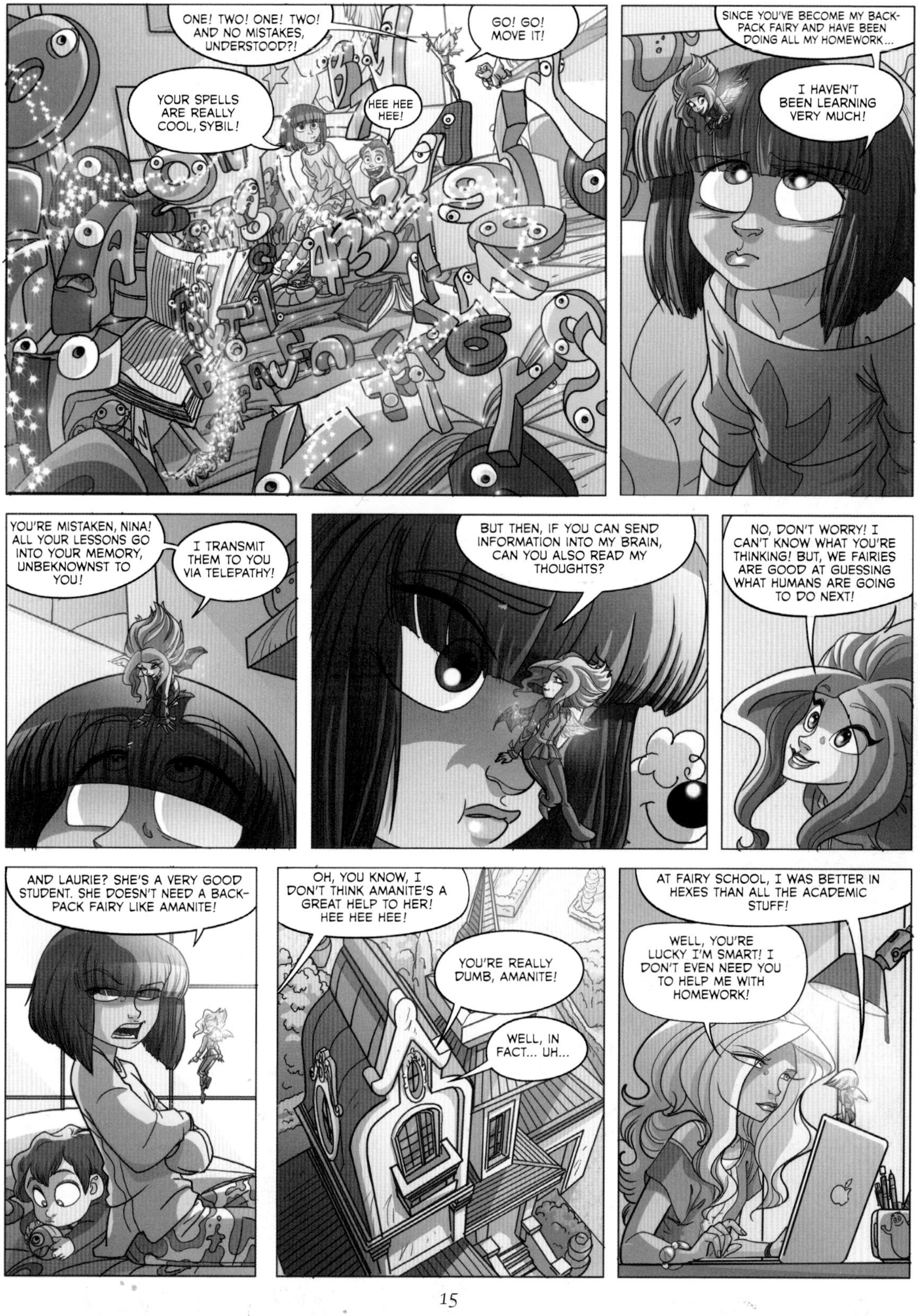
ONE! TWO! ONE! TWO! AND NO MISTAKES, UNDERSTOOD?!
GO! GO! MOVE IT!
YOUR SPELLS ARE REALLY COOL, SYBIL!
HEE HEE HEE!
SINCE YOU'VE BECOME MY BACK-PACK FAIRY AND HAVE BEEN DOING ALL MY HOMEWORK...
I HAVEN'T BEEN LEARNING VERY MUCH!
YOU'RE MISTAKEN, NINA! ALL YOUR LESSONS GO INTO YOUR MEMORY, UNBEKNOWNST TO YOU!
I TRANSMIT THEM TO YOU VIA TELEPATHY!
BUT THEN, IF YOU CAN SEND INFORMATION INTO MY BRAIN, CAN YOU ALSO READ MY THOUGHTS?
NO, DON'T WORRY! I CAN'T KNOW WHAT YOU'RE THINKING! BUT, WE FAIRIES ARE GOOD AT GUESSING WHAT HUMANS ARE GOING TO DO NEXT!
AND LAURIE? SHE'S A VERY GOOD STUDENT. SHE DOESN'T NEED A BACK-PACK FAIRY LIKE AMANITE!
OH, YOU KNOW, I DON'T THINK AMANITE'S A GREAT HELP TO HER! HEE HEE HEE!
YOU'RE REALLY DUMB, AMANITE!
WELL, IN FACT... UH...
AT FAIRY SCHOOL, I WAS BETTER IN HEXES THAN ALL THE ACADEMIC STUFF!
WELL, YOU'RE LUCKY I'M SMART! I DON'T EVEN NEED YOU TO HELP ME WITH HOMEWORK!

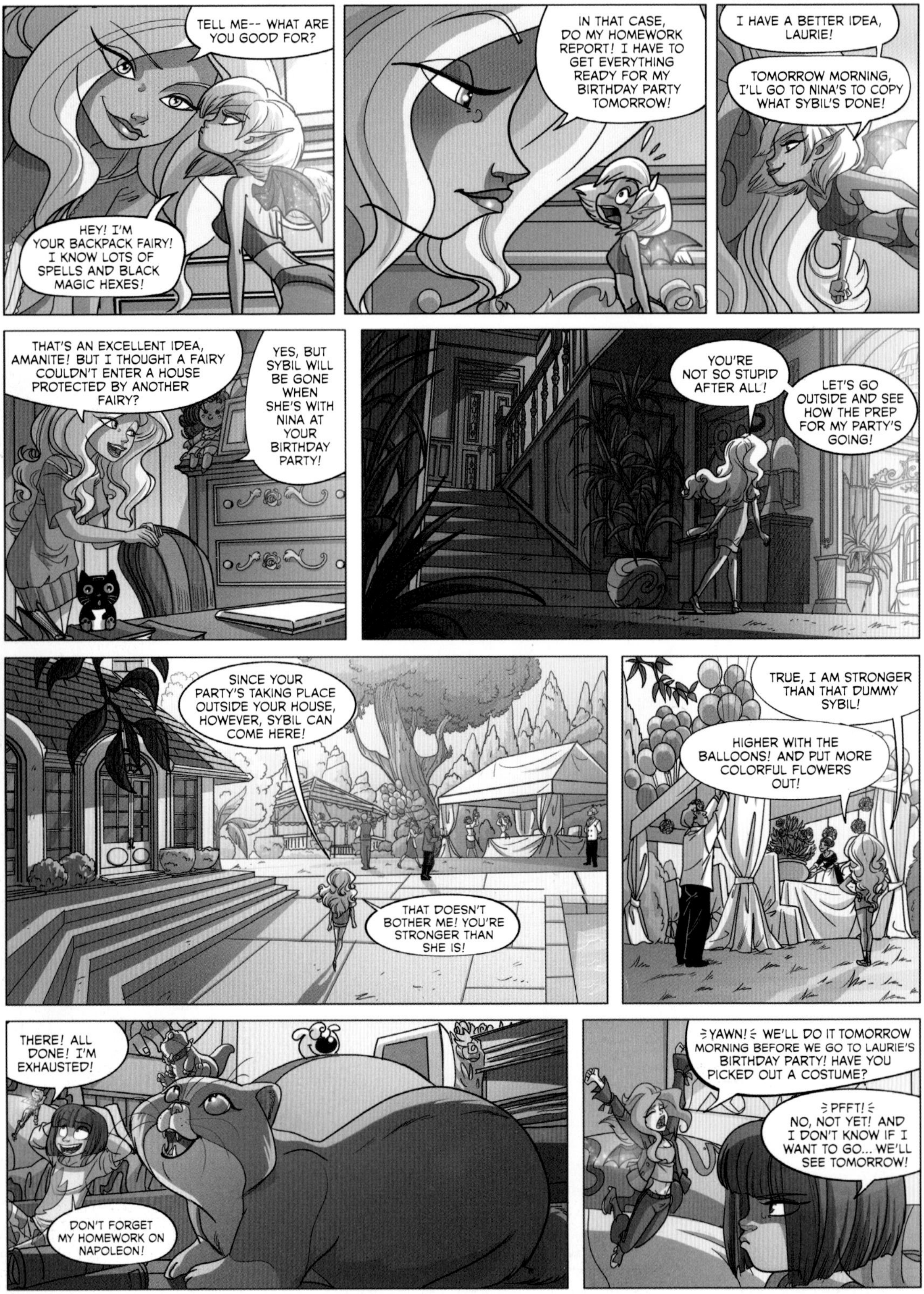
TELL ME-- WHAT ARE YOU GOOD FOR?
HEY! I'M YOUR BACKPACK FAIRY! I KNOW LOTS OF SPELLS AND BLACK MAGIC HEXES!
IN THAT CASE, DO MY HOMEWORK REPORT! I HAVE TO GET EVERYTHING READY FOR MY BIRTHDAY PARTY TOMORROW!
I HAVE A BETTER IDEA, LAURIE!
TOMORROW MORNING, I'LL GO TO NINA'S TO COPY WHAT SYBIL'S DONE!
THAT'S AN EXCELLENT IDEA, AMANITE! BUT I THOUGHT A FAIRY COULDN'T ENTER A HOUSE PROTECTED BY ANOTHER FAIRY?
YES, BUT SYBIL WILL BE GONE WHEN SHE'S WITH NINA AT YOUR BIRTHDAY PARTY!
YOU'RE NOT SO STUPID AFTER ALL!
LET'S GO OUTSIDE AND SEE HOW THE PREP FOR MY PARTY'S GOING!
SINCE YOUR PARTY'S TAKING PLACE OUTSIDE YOUR HOUSE, HOWEVER, SYBIL CAN COME HERE!
THAT DOESN'T BOTHER ME! YOU'RE STRONGER THAN SHE IS!
TRUE, I AM STRONGER THAN THAT DUMMY SYBIL!
HIGHER WITH THE BALLOONS! AND PUT MORE COLORFUL FLOWERS OUT!
THERE! ALL DONE! I'M EXHAUSTED!
DON'T FORGET MY HOMEWORK ON NAPOLEON!
≷YAWN!≶ WE'LL DO IT TOMORROW MORNING BEFORE WE GO TO LAURIE'S BIRTHDAY PARTY! HAVE YOU PICKED OUT A COSTUME?
≷PFFT!≶ NO, NOT YET! AND I DON'T KNOW IF I WANT TO GO... WE'LL SEE TOMORROW!

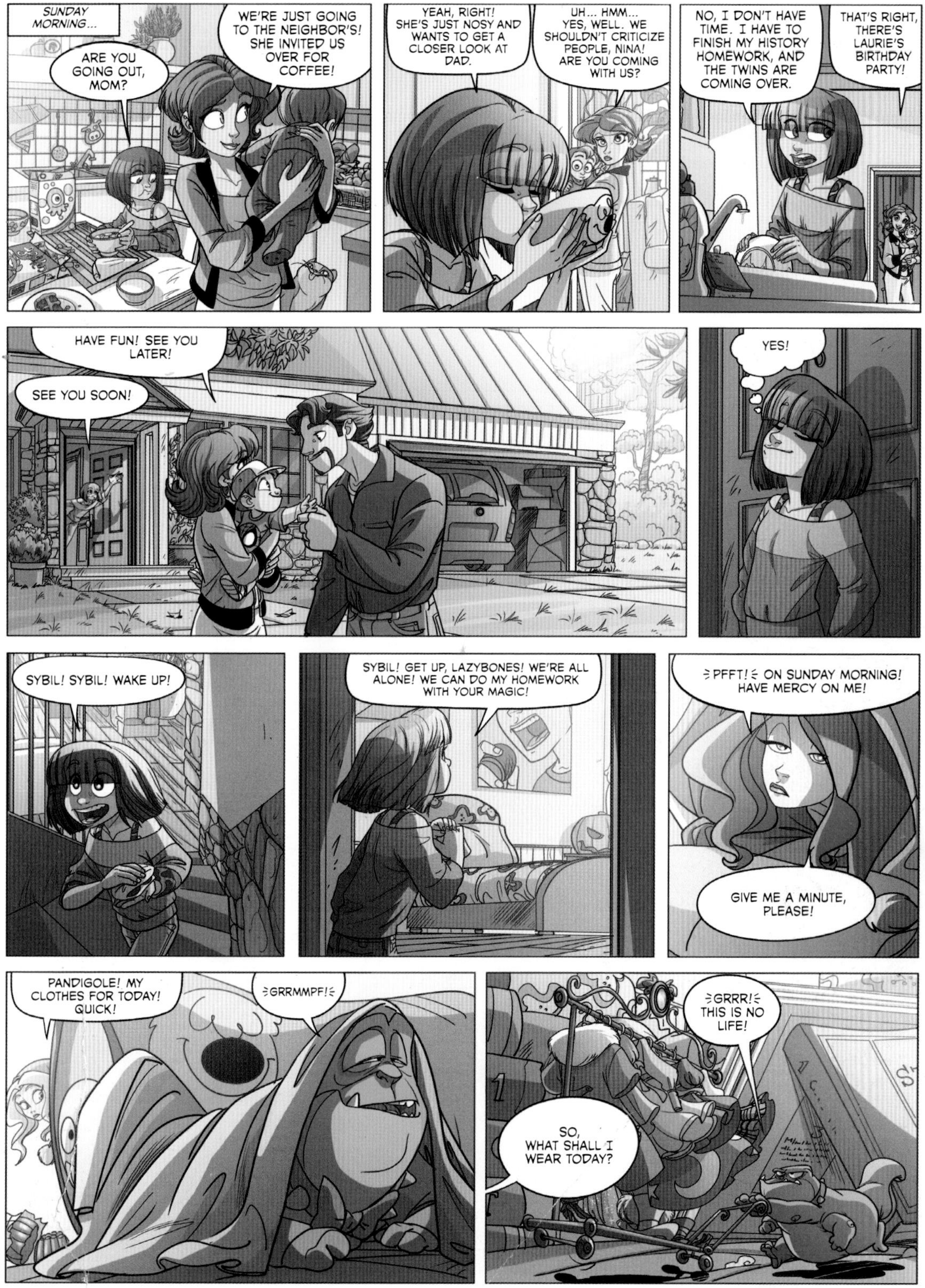
SUNDAY MORNING...
ARE YOU GOING OUT, MOM?
WE'RE JUST GOING TO THE NEIGHBOR'S! SHE INVITED US OVER FOR COFFEE!
YEAH, RIGHT! SHE'S JUST NOSY AND WANTS TO GET A CLOSER LOOK AT DAD.
UH... HMM... YES, WELL. WE SHOULDN'T CRITICIZE PEOPLE, NINA! ARE YOU COMING WITH US?
NO, I DON'T HAVE TIME. I HAVE TO FINISH MY HISTORY HOMEWORK, AND THE TWINS ARE COMING OVER.
THAT'S RIGHT, THERE'S LAURIE'S BIRTHDAY PARTY!
HAVE FUN! SEE YOU LATER!
SEE YOU SOON!
YES!
SYBIL! SYBIL! WAKE UP!
SYBIL! GET UP, LAZYBONES! WE'RE ALL ALONE! WE CAN DO MY HOMEWORK WITH YOUR MAGIC!
PFFT! ON SUNDAY MORNING! HAVE MERCY ON ME!
GIVE ME A MINUTE, PLEASE!
PANDIGOLE! MY CLOTHES FOR TODAY! QUICK!
GRRMMPF!
GRRR! THIS IS NO LIFE!
SO, WHAT SHALL I WEAR TODAY?

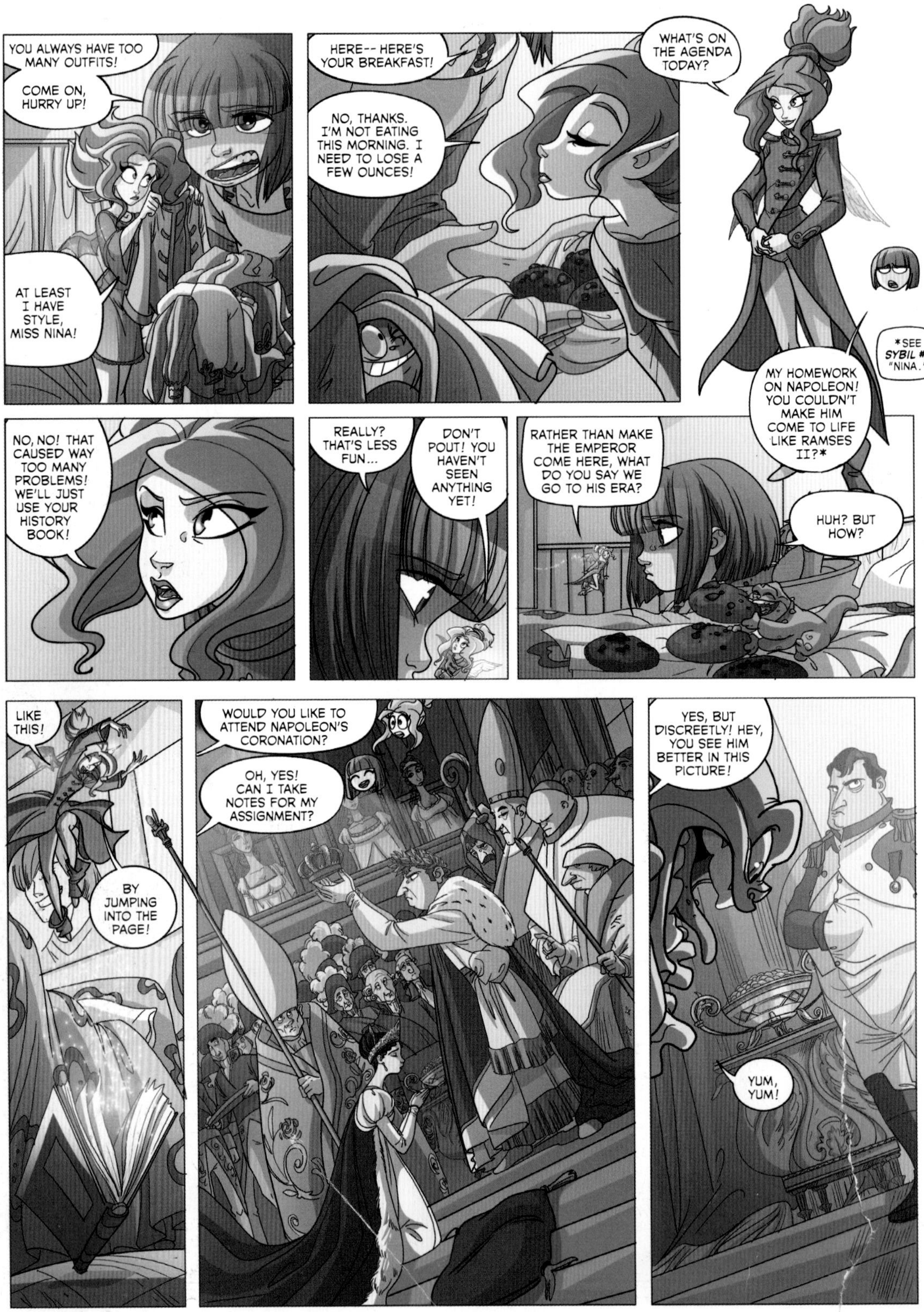
YOU ALWAYS HAVE TOO MANY OUTFITS!
COME ON, HURRY UP!
AT LEAST I HAVE STYLE, MISS NINA!
HERE-- HERE'S YOUR BREAKFAST!
NO, THANKS. I'M NOT EATING THIS MORNING. I NEED TO LOSE A FEW OUNCES!
WHAT'S ON THE AGENDA TODAY?
MY HOMEWORK ON NAPOLEON! YOU COULDN'T MAKE HIM COME TO LIFE LIKE RAMSES II?*
*SEE SYBIL #1 "NINA."
NO, NO! THAT CAUSED WAY TOO MANY PROBLEMS! WE'LL JUST USE YOUR HISTORY BOOK!
REALLY? THAT'S LESS FUN...
DON'T POUT! YOU HAVEN'T SEEN ANYTHING YET!
RATHER THAN MAKE THE EMPEROR COME HERE, WHAT DO YOU SAY WE GO TO HIS ERA?
HUH? BUT HOW?
LIKE THIS!
BY JUMPING INTO THE PAGE!
WOULD YOU LIKE TO ATTEND NAPOLEON'S CORONATION?
OH, YES! CAN I TAKE NOTES FOR MY ASSIGNMENT?
YES, BUT DISCREETLY! HEY, YOU SEE HIM BETTER IN THIS PICTURE!
YUM, YUM!

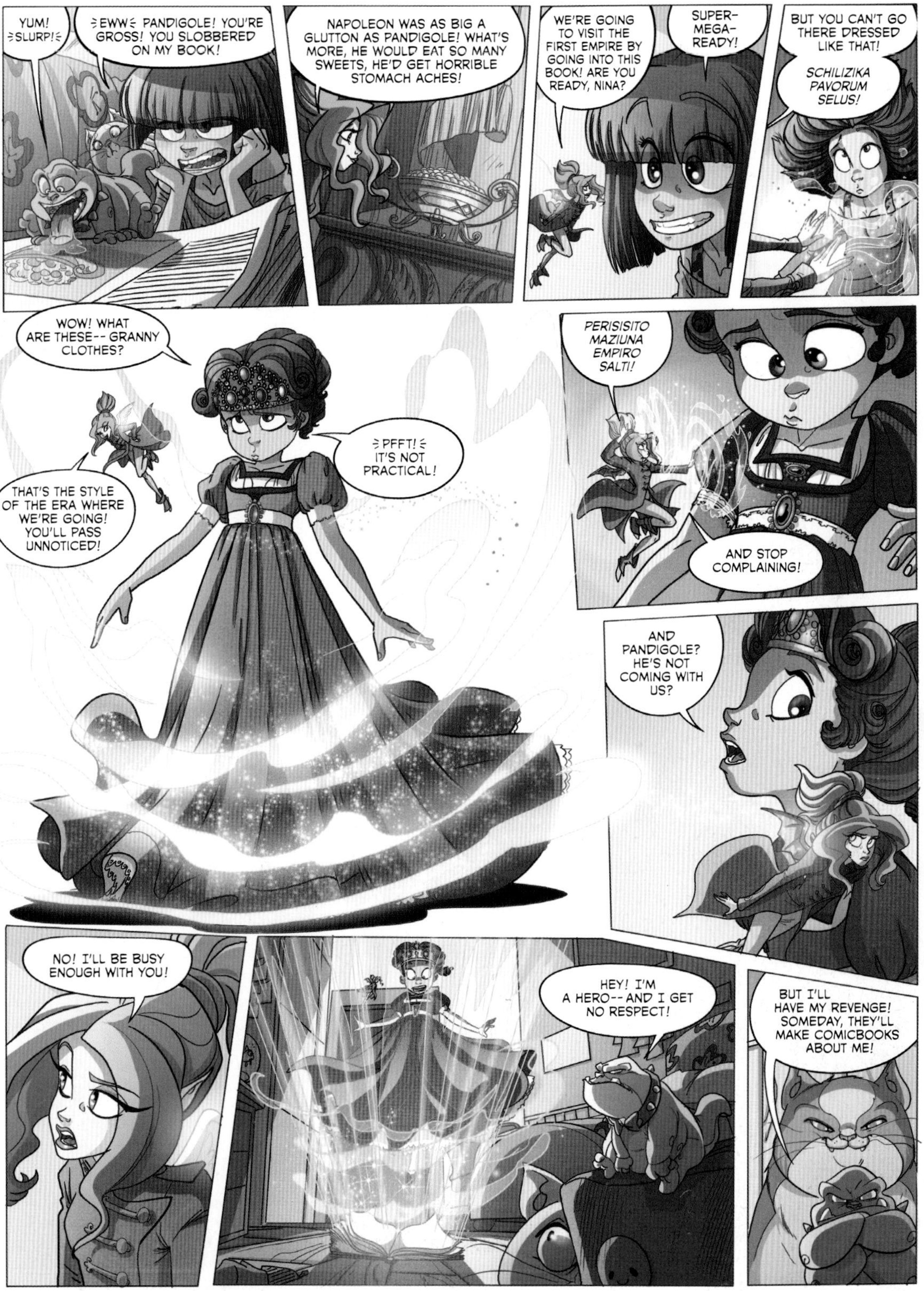
YUM! ≷SLURP!≶
≷EWW≶ PANDIGOLE! YOU'RE GROSS! YOU SLOBBERED ON MY BOOK!
NAPOLEON WAS AS BIG A GLUTTON AS PANDIGOLE! WHAT'S MORE, HE WOULD EAT SO MANY SWEETS, HE'D GET HORRIBLE STOMACH ACHES!
WE'RE GOING TO VISIT THE FIRST EMPIRE BY GOING INTO THIS BOOK! ARE YOU READY, NINA?
SUPER-MEGA-READY!
BUT YOU CAN'T GO THERE DRESSED LIKE THAT!
SCHILIZIKA PAVORUM SELUS!
WOW! WHAT ARE THESE-- GRANNY CLOTHES?
THAT'S THE STYLE OF THE ERA WHERE WE'RE GOING! YOU'LL PASS UNNOTICED!
≷PFFT!≶ IT'S NOT PRACTICAL!
PERISISITO MAZIUNA EMPIRO SALTI!
AND STOP COMPLAINING!
AND PANDIGOLE? HE'S NOT COMING WITH US?
NO! I'LL BE BUSY ENOUGH WITH YOU!
HEY! I'M A HERO-- AND I GET NO RESPECT!
BUT I'LL HAVE MY REVENGE! SOMEDAY, THEY'LL MAKE COMICBOOKS ABOUT ME!

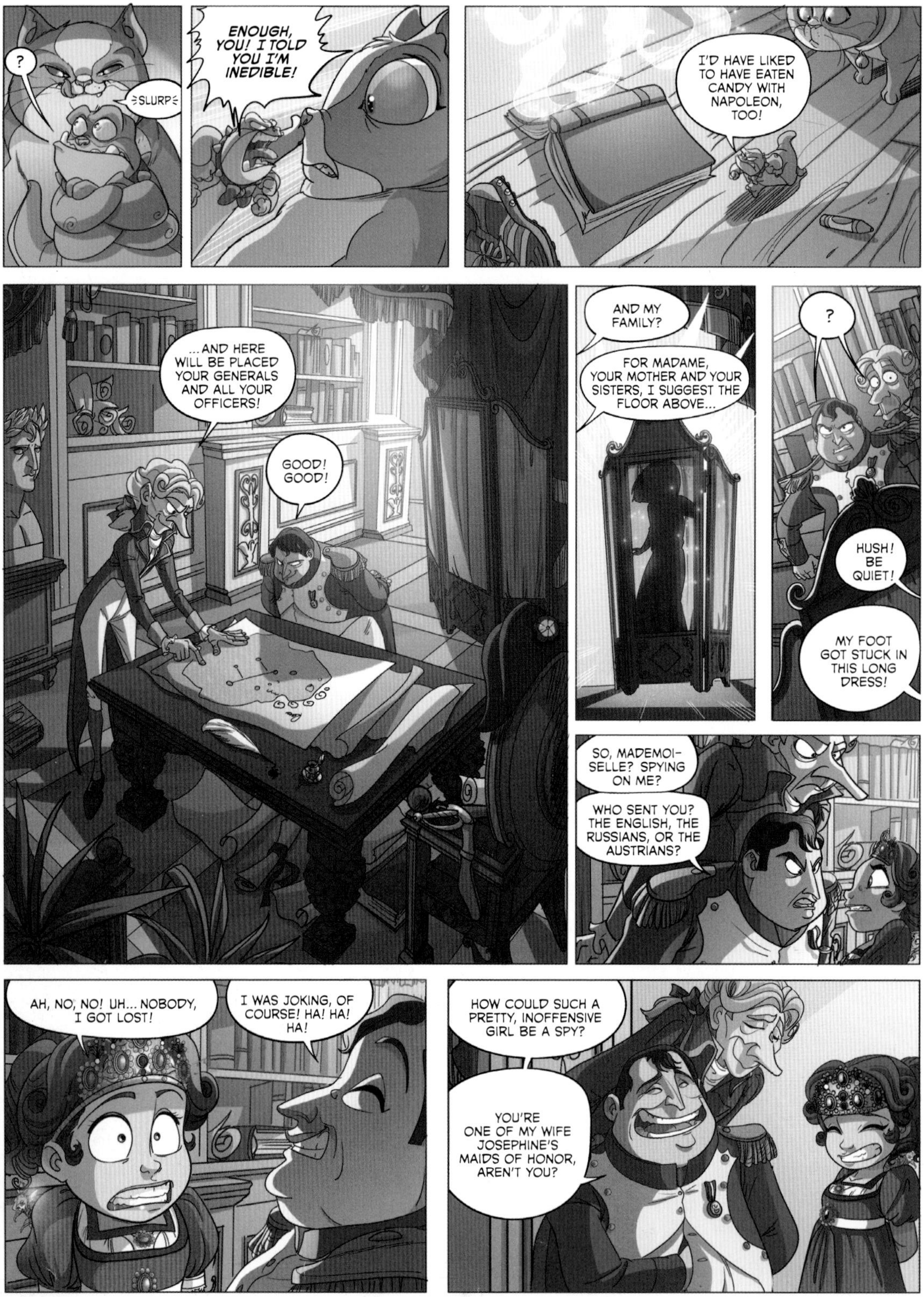
?
SLURP
ENOUGH, YOU! I TOLD YOU I'M INEDIBLE!
I'D HAVE LIKED TO HAVE EATEN CANDY WITH NAPOLEON, TOO!
...AND HERE WILL BE PLACED YOUR GENERALS AND ALL YOUR OFFICERS!
GOOD! GOOD!
AND MY FAMILY?
FOR MADAME, YOUR MOTHER AND YOUR SISTERS, I SUGGEST THE FLOOR ABOVE...
?
HUSH! BE QUIET!
MY FOOT GOT STUCK IN THIS LONG DRESS!
SO, MADEMOI-SELLE? SPYING ON ME?
WHO SENT YOU? THE ENGLISH, THE RUSSIANS, OR THE AUSTRIANS?
AH, NO, NO! UH... NOBODY, I GOT LOST!
I WAS JOKING, OF COURSE! HA! HA! HA!
HOW COULD SUCH A PRETTY, INOFFENSIVE GIRL BE A SPY?
YOU'RE ONE OF MY WIFE JOSEPHINE'S MAIDS OF HONOR, AREN'T YOU?

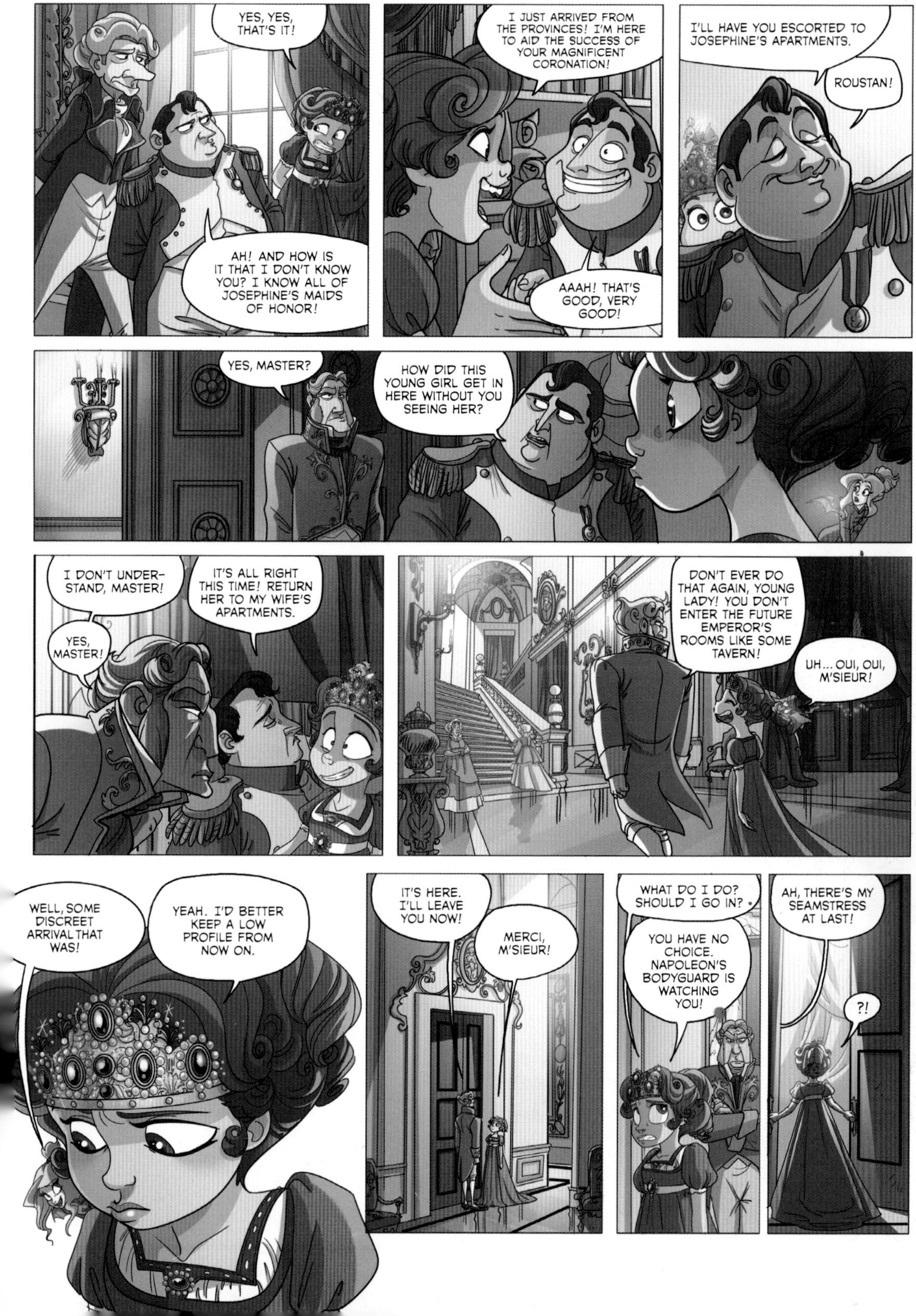

YES, YES, THAT'S IT!
AH! AND HOW IS IT THAT I DON'T KNOW YOU? I KNOW ALL OF JOSEPHINE'S MAIDS OF HONOR!
I JUST ARRIVED FROM THE PROVINCES! I'M HERE TO AID THE SUCCESS OF YOUR MAGNIFICENT CORONATION!
AAAH! THAT'S GOOD, VERY GOOD!
I'LL HAVE YOU ESCORTED TO JOSEPHINE'S APARTMENTS.
ROUSTAN!
YES, MASTER?
HOW DID THIS YOUNG GIRL GET IN HERE WITHOUT YOU SEEING HER?
I DON'T UNDER-STAND, MASTER!
IT'S ALL RIGHT THIS TIME! RETURN HER TO MY WIFE'S APARTMENTS.
YES, MASTER!
DON'T EVER DO THAT AGAIN, YOUNG LADY! YOU DON'T ENTER THE FUTURE EMPEROR'S ROOMS LIKE SOME TAVERN!
UH... OUI, OUI, M'SIEUR!
WELL, SOME DISCREET ARRIVAL THAT WAS!
YEAH. I'D BETTER KEEP A LOW PROFILE FROM NOW ON.
IT'S HERE. I'LL LEAVE YOU NOW!
MERCI, M'SIEUR!
WHAT DO I DO? SHOULD I GO IN?
YOU HAVE NO CHOICE. NAPOLEON'S BODYGUARD IS WATCHING YOU!
AH, THERE'S MY SEAMSTRESS AT LAST!
?!

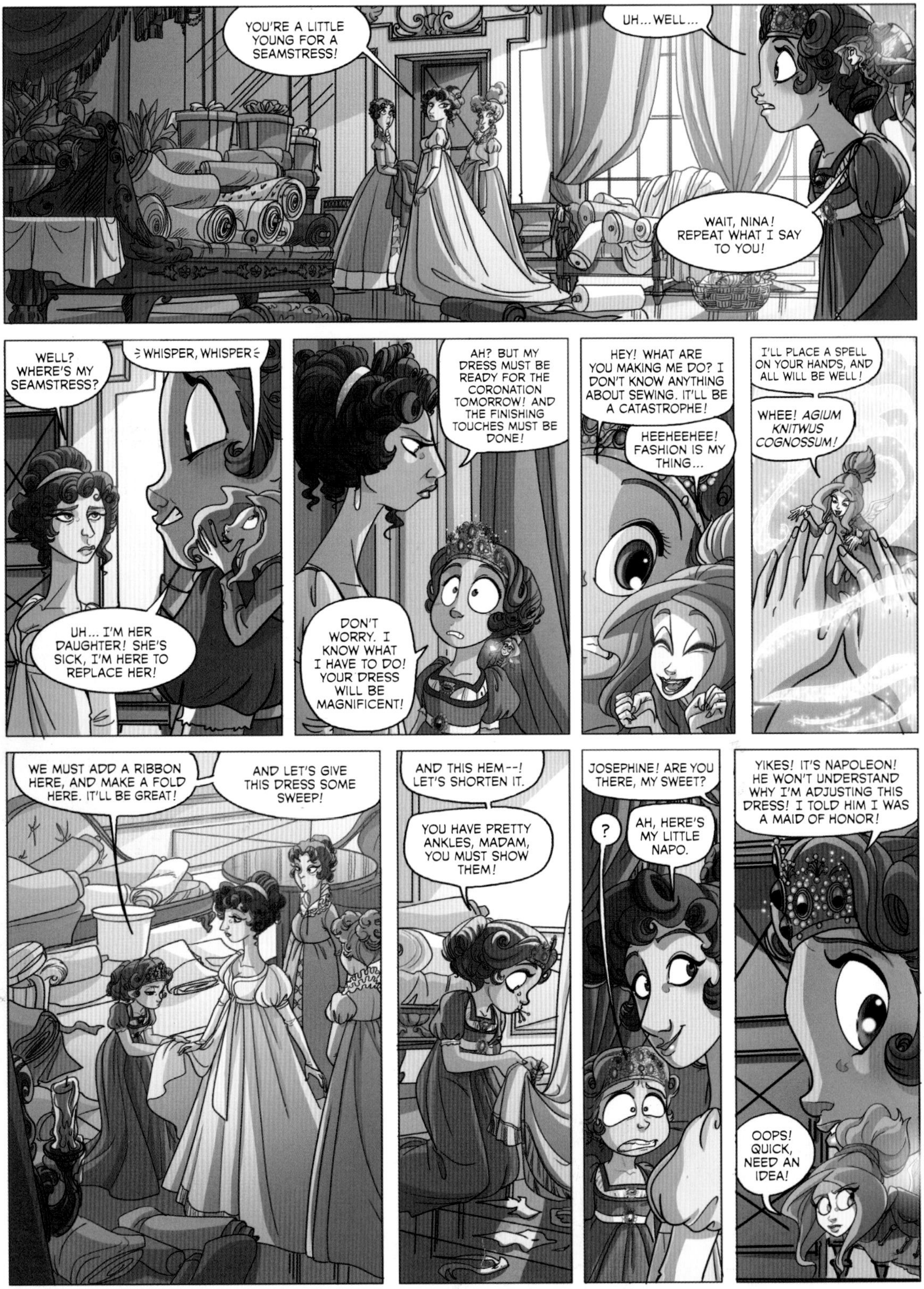
YOU'RE A LITTLE YOUNG FOR A SEAMSTRESS!
UH... WELL...
WAIT, NINA! REPEAT WHAT I SAY TO YOU!
WELL? WHERE'S MY SEAMSTRESS?
WHISPER, WHISPER
UH... I'M HER DAUGHTER! SHE'S SICK, I'M HERE TO REPLACE HER!
AH? BUT MY DRESS MUST BE READY FOR THE CORONATION TOMORROW! AND THE FINISHING TOUCHES MUST BE DONE!
DON'T WORRY. I KNOW WHAT I HAVE TO DO! YOUR DRESS WILL BE MAGNIFICENT!
HEY! WHAT ARE YOU MAKING ME DO? I DON'T KNOW ANYTHING ABOUT SEWING. IT'LL BE A CATASTROPHE!
HEEHEEHEE! FASHION IS MY THING...
I'LL PLACE A SPELL ON YOUR HANDS, AND ALL WILL BE WELL!
WHEE! *AGIUM KNITWUS COGNOSSUM!*
WE MUST ADD A RIBBON HERE, AND MAKE A FOLD HERE. IT'LL BE GREAT!
AND LET'S GIVE THIS DRESS SOME SWEEP!
AND THIS HEM--! LET'S SHORTEN IT.
YOU HAVE PRETTY ANKLES, MADAM, YOU MUST SHOW THEM!
JOSEPHINE! ARE YOU THERE, MY SWEET?
?
AH, HERE'S MY LITTLE NAPO.
YIKES! IT'S NAPOLEON! HE WON'T UNDERSTAND WHY I'M ADJUSTING THIS DRESS! I TOLD HIM I WAS A MAID OF HONOR!
OOPS! QUICK, NEED AN IDEA!

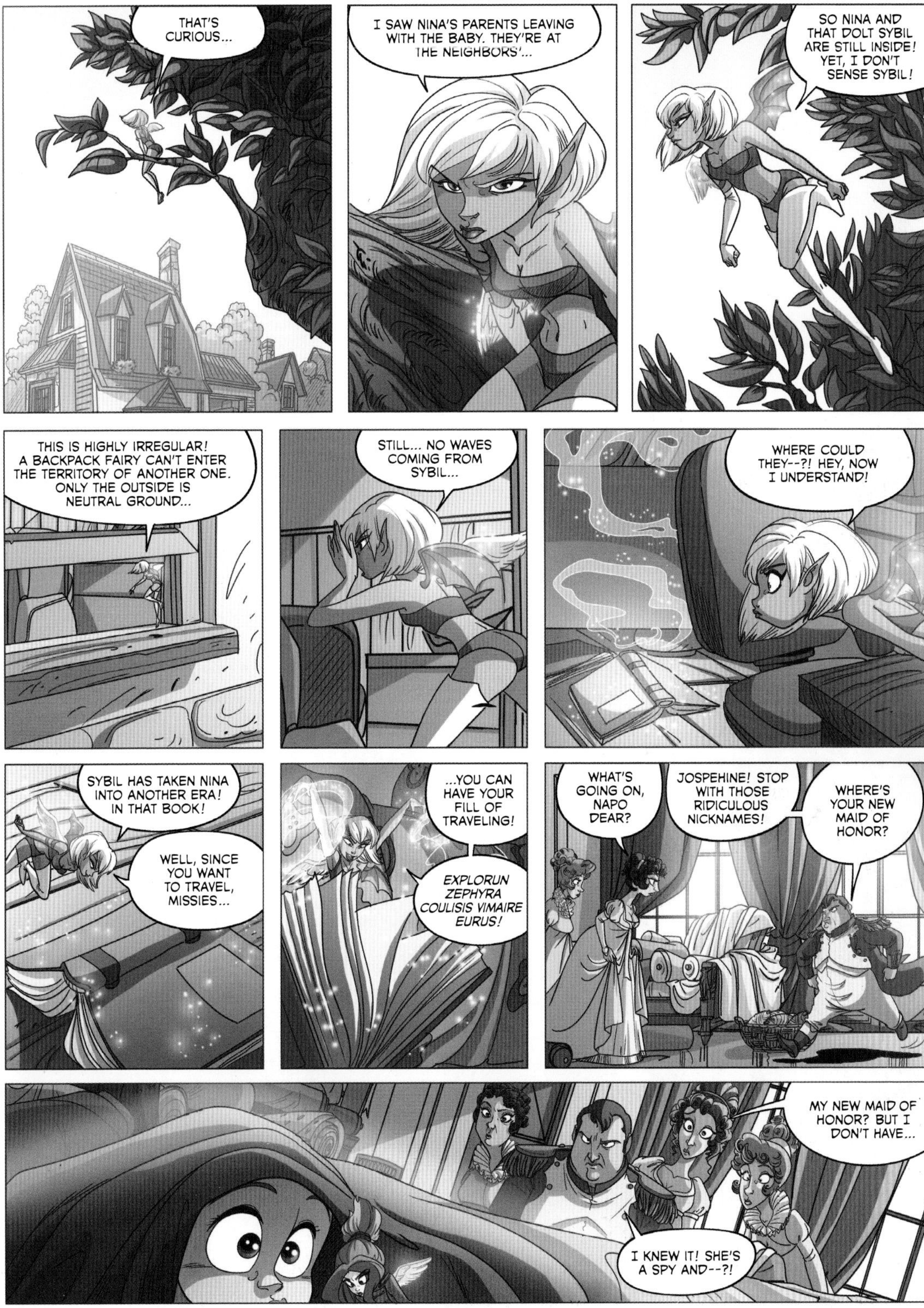
THAT'S CURIOUS...
I SAW NINA'S PARENTS LEAVING WITH THE BABY. THEY'RE AT THE NEIGHBORS'...
SO NINA AND THAT DOLT SYBIL ARE STILL INSIDE! YET, I DON'T SENSE SYBIL!
THIS IS HIGHLY IRREGULAR! A BACKPACK FAIRY CAN'T ENTER THE TERRITORY OF ANOTHER ONE. ONLY THE OUTSIDE IS NEUTRAL GROUND...
STILL... NO WAVES COMING FROM SYBIL...
WHERE COULD THEY--?! HEY, NOW I UNDERSTAND!
SYBIL HAS TAKEN NINA INTO ANOTHER ERA! IN THAT BOOK!
WELL, SINCE YOU WANT TO TRAVEL, MISSIES...
...YOU CAN HAVE YOUR FILL OF TRAVELING!
EXPLORUN ZEPHYRA COULISIS VIMAIRE EURUS!
WHAT'S GOING ON, NAPO DEAR?
JOSPEHINE! STOP WITH THOSE RIDICULOUS NICKNAMES!
WHERE'S YOUR NEW MAID OF HONOR?
MY NEW MAID OF HONOR? BUT I DON'T HAVE...
I KNEW IT! SHE'S A SPY AND--?!

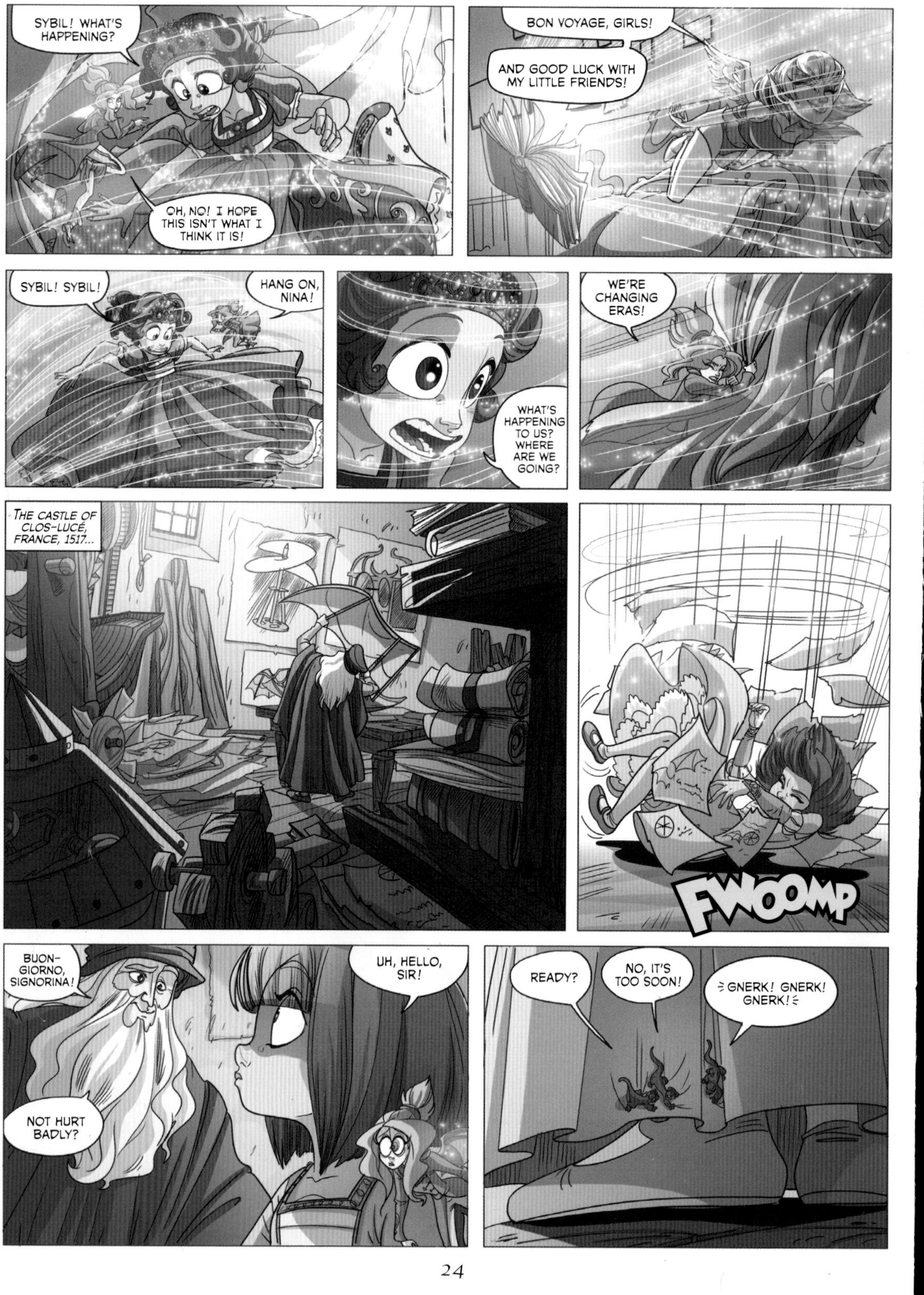
SYBIL! WHAT'S HAPPENING?
OH, NO! I HOPE THIS ISN'T WHAT I THINK IT IS!
BON VOYAGE, GIRLS!
AND GOOD LUCK WITH MY LITTLE FRIENDS!
SYBIL! SYBIL!
HANG ON, NINA!
WHAT'S HAPPENING TO US? WHERE ARE WE GOING?
WE'RE CHANGING ERAS!
THE CASTLE OF CLOS-LUCÉ, FRANCE, 1517...
FWOOMP
BUON-GIORNO, SIGNORINA!
UH, HELLO, SIR!
NOT HURT BADLY?
READY?
NO, IT'S TOO SOON!
GNERK! GNERK! GNERK!

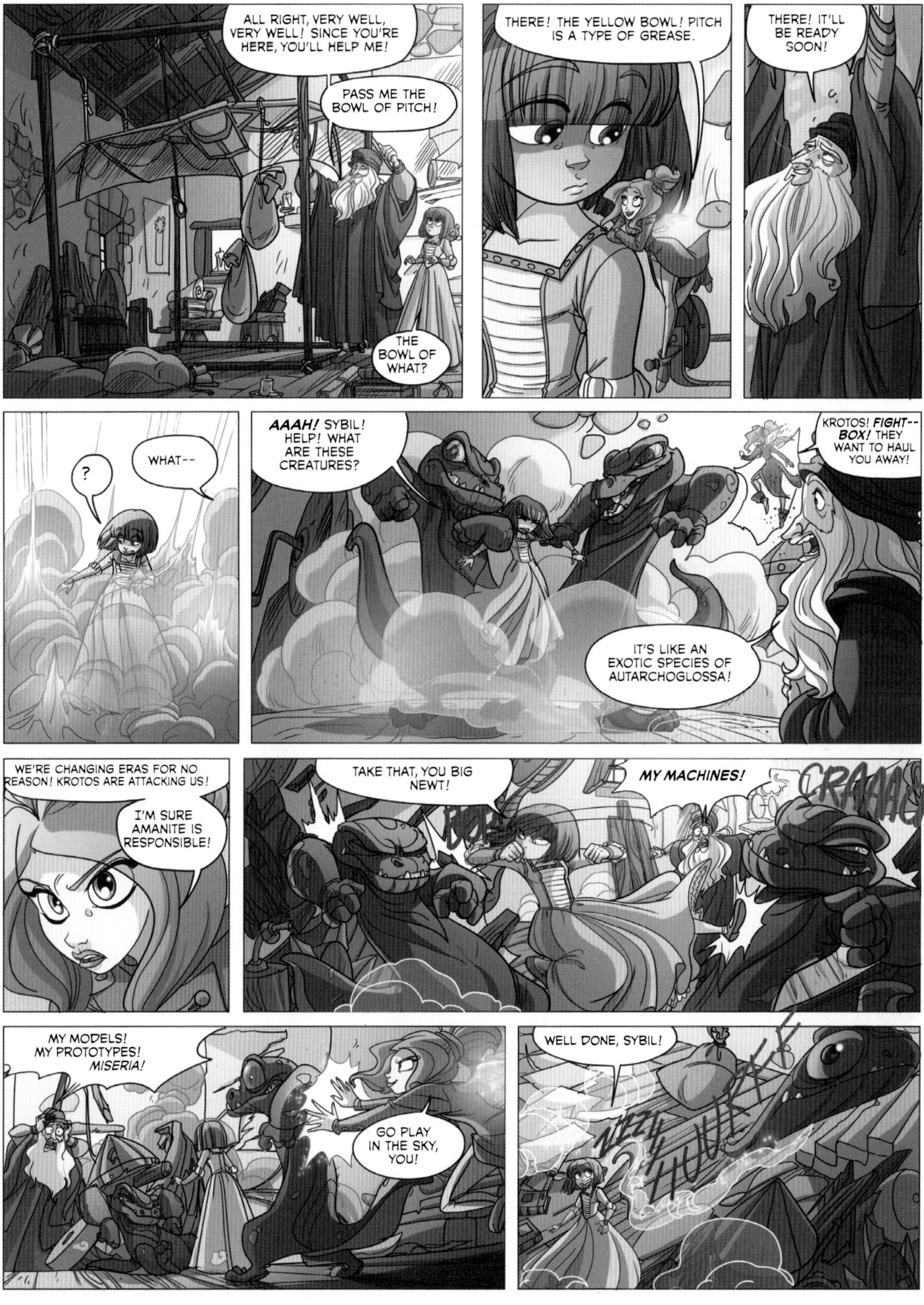
ALL RIGHT, VERY WELL, VERY WELL! SINCE YOU'RE HERE, YOU'LL HELP ME!
PASS ME THE BOWL OF PITCH!
THE BOWL OF WHAT?
THERE! THE YELLOW BOWL! PITCH IS A TYPE OF GREASE.
THERE! IT'LL BE READY SOON!
?
WHAT--
AAAH! SYBIL! HELP! WHAT ARE THESE CREATURES?
KROTOS! FIGHT--BOX! THEY WANT TO HAUL YOU AWAY!
IT'S LIKE AN EXOTIC SPECIES OF AUTARCHOGLOSSA!
WE'RE CHANGING ERAS FOR NO REASON! KROTOS ARE ATTACKING US!
I'M SURE AMANITE IS RESPONSIBLE!
TAKE THAT, YOU BIG NEWT!
MY MACHINES!
CRAAACK
MY MODELS! MY PROTOTYPES! MISERIA!
GO PLAY IN THE SKY, YOU!
WELL DONE, SYBIL!

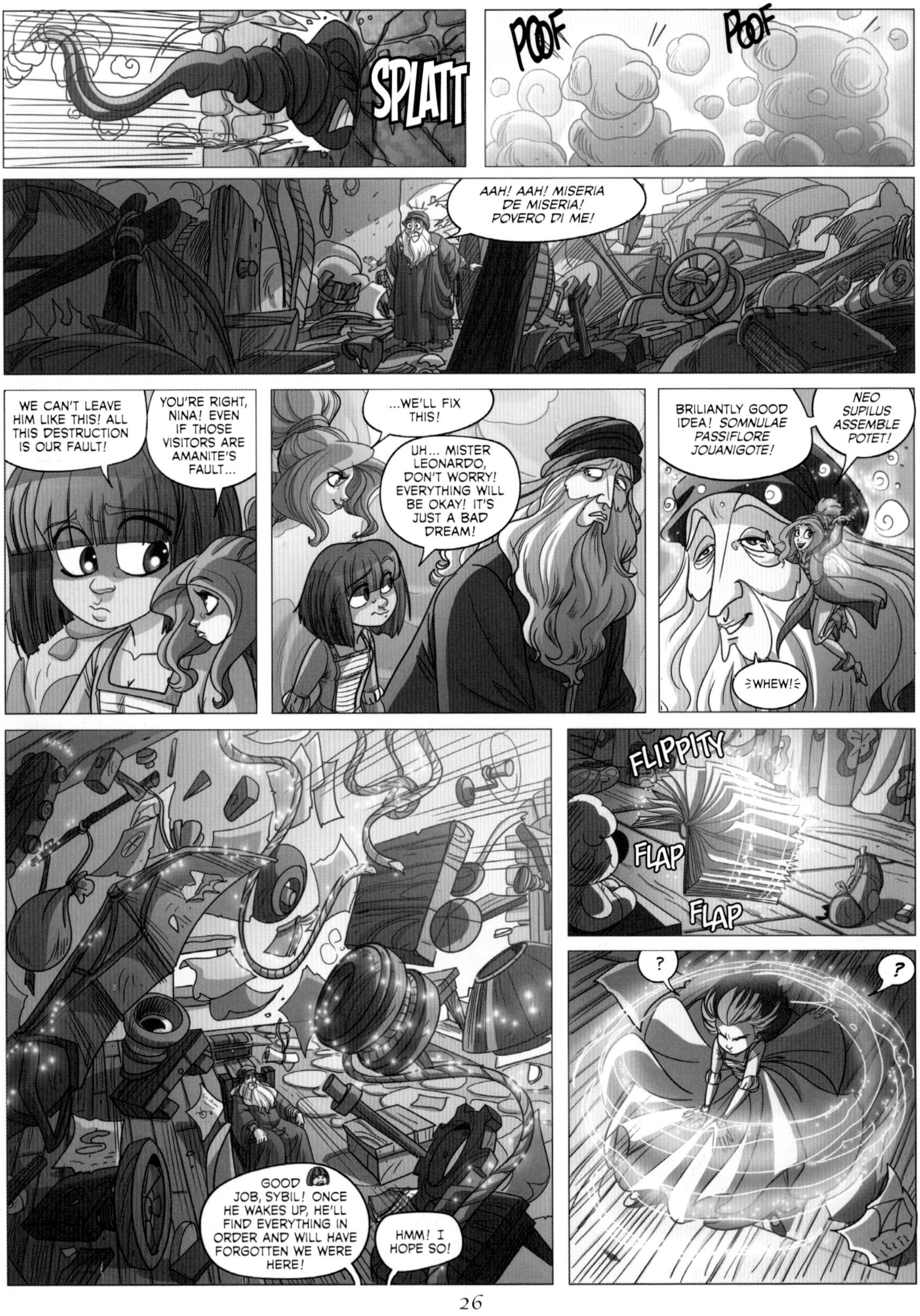
SPLATT
POOF
POOF
AAH! AAH! MISERIA DE MISERIA! POVERO DI ME!
WE CAN'T LEAVE HIM LIKE THIS! ALL THIS DESTRUCTION IS OUR FAULT!
YOU'RE RIGHT, NINA! EVEN IF THOSE VISITORS ARE AMANITE'S FAULT...
...WE'LL FIX THIS!
UH... MISTER LEONARDO, DON'T WORRY! EVERYTHING WILL BE OKAY! IT'S JUST A BAD DREAM!
BRILIANTLY GOOD IDEA! SOMNULAE PASSIFLORE JOUANIGOTE!
NEO SUPILUS ASSEMBLE POTET!
WHEW!
FLIPPITY
FLAP
FLAP
?
?
GOOD JOB, SYBIL! ONCE HE WAKES UP, HE'LL FIND EVERYTHING IN ORDER AND WILL HAVE FORGOTTEN WE WERE HERE!
HMM! I HOPE SO!

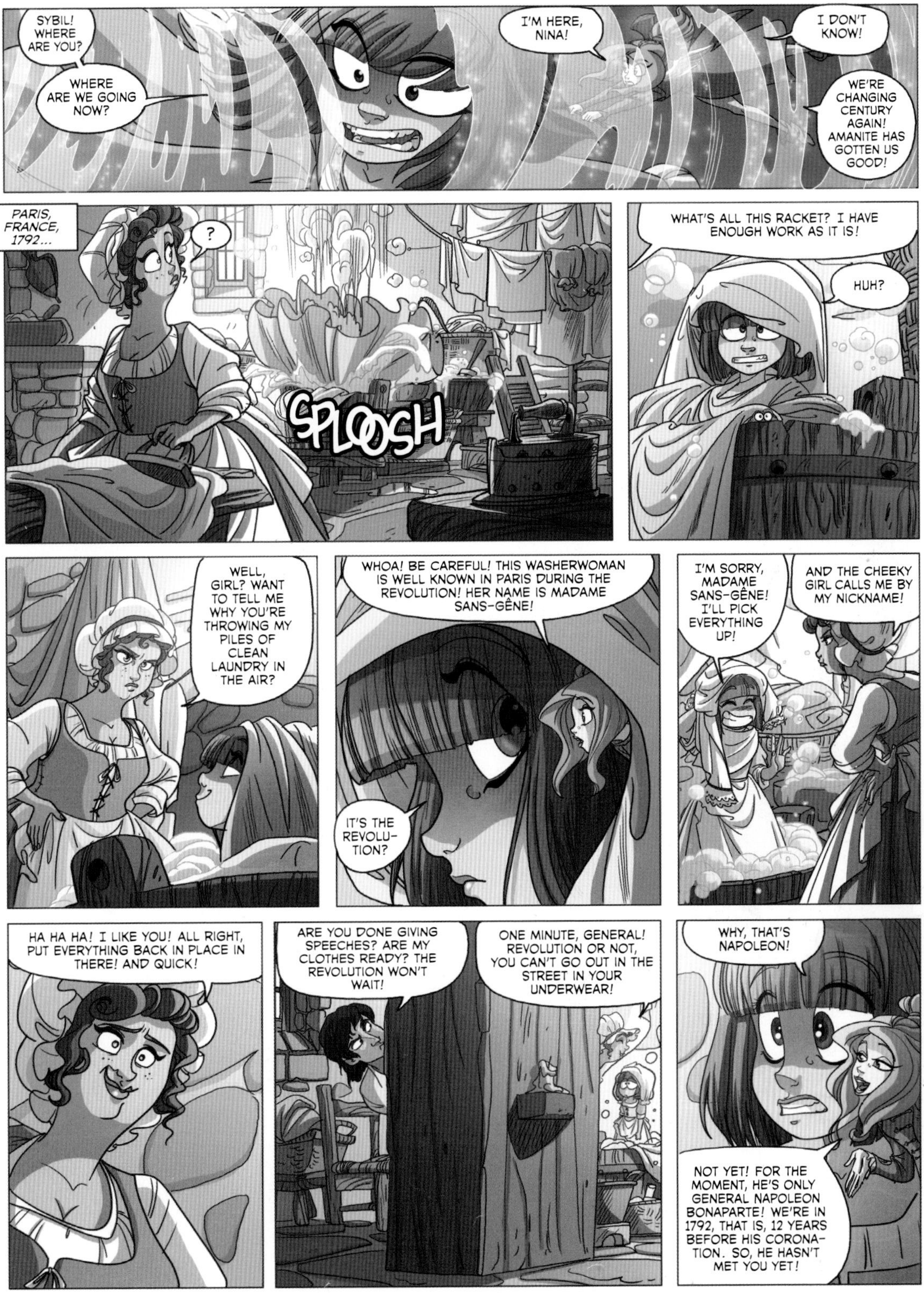
SYBIL! WHERE ARE YOU?
WHERE ARE WE GOING NOW?
I'M HERE, NINA!
I DON'T KNOW!
WE'RE CHANGING CENTURY AGAIN! AMANITE HAS GOTTEN US GOOD!
PARIS, FRANCE, 1792...
?
SPLOOSH
WHAT'S ALL THIS RACKET? I HAVE ENOUGH WORK AS IT IS!
HUH?
WELL, GIRL? WANT TO TELL ME WHY YOU'RE THROWING MY PILES OF CLEAN LAUNDRY IN THE AIR?
WHOA! BE CAREFUL! THIS WASHERWOMAN IS WELL KNOWN IN PARIS DURING THE REVOLUTION! HER NAME IS MADAME SANS-GÊNE!
IT'S THE REVOLU-TION?
I'M SORRY, MADAME SANS-GÊNE! I'LL PICK EVERYTHING UP!
AND THE CHEEKY GIRL CALLS ME BY MY NICKNAME!
HA HA HA! I LIKE YOU! ALL RIGHT, PUT EVERYTHING BACK IN PLACE IN THERE! AND QUICK!
ARE YOU DONE GIVING SPEECHES? ARE MY CLOTHES READY? THE REVOLUTION WON'T WAIT!
ONE MINUTE, GENERAL! REVOLUTION OR NOT, YOU CAN'T GO OUT IN THE STREET IN YOUR UNDERWEAR!
WHY, THAT'S NAPOLEON!
NOT YET! FOR THE MOMENT, HE'S ONLY GENERAL NAPOLEON BONAPARTE! WE'RE IN 1792, THAT IS, 12 YEARS BEFORE HIS CORONA-TION. SO, HE HASN'T MET YOU YET!

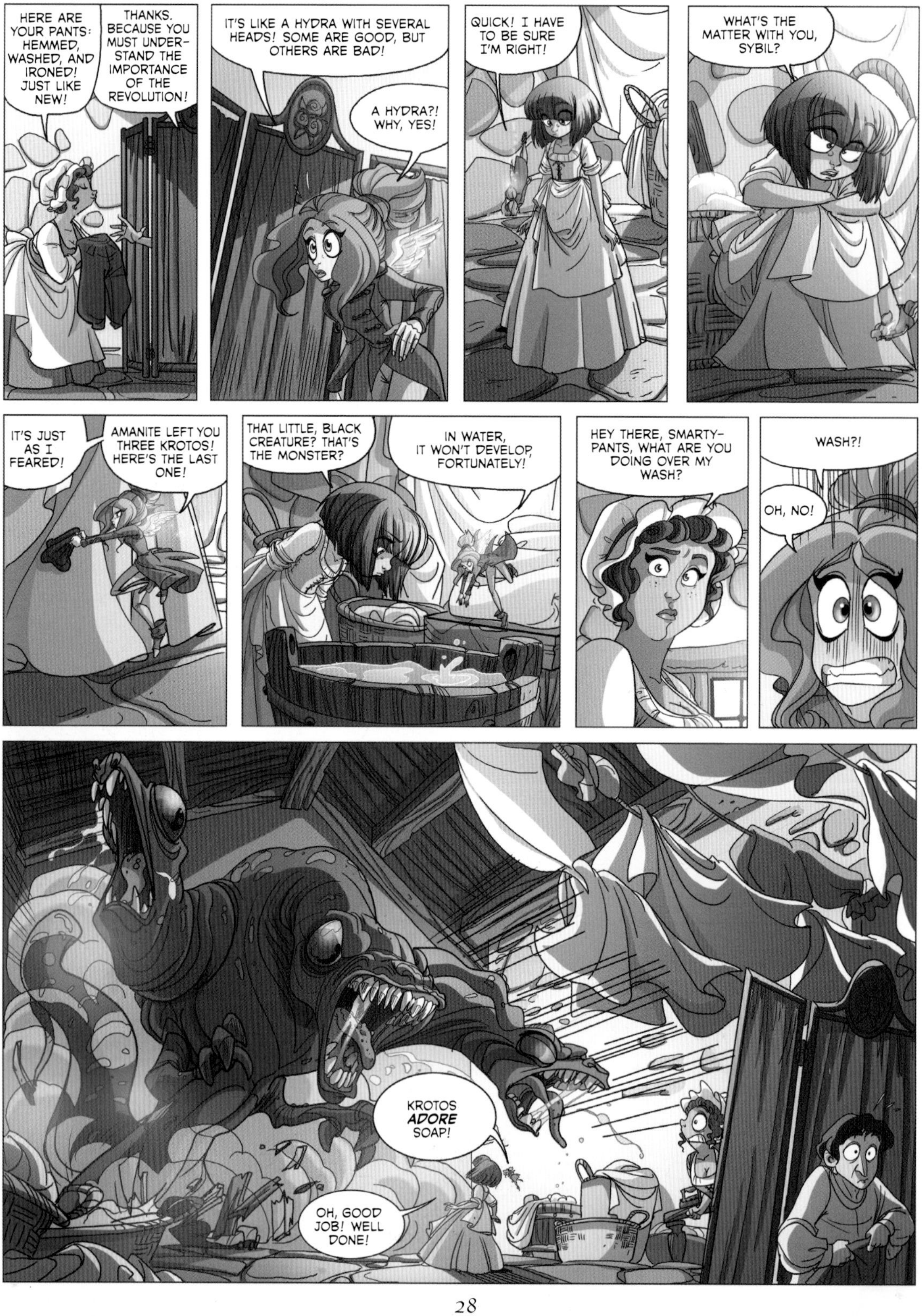
HERE ARE YOUR PANTS: HEMMED, WASHED, AND IRONED! JUST LIKE NEW!
THANKS. BECAUSE YOU MUST UNDER-STAND THE IMPORTANCE OF THE REVOLUTION!
IT'S LIKE A HYDRA WITH SEVERAL HEADS! SOME ARE GOOD, BUT OTHERS ARE BAD!
A HYDRA?! WHY, YES!
QUICK! I HAVE TO BE SURE I'M RIGHT!
WHAT'S THE MATTER WITH YOU, SYBIL?
IT'S JUST AS I FEARED!
AMANITE LEFT YOU THREE KROTOS! HERE'S THE LAST ONE!
THAT LITTLE, BLACK CREATURE? THAT'S THE MONSTER?
IN WATER, IT WON'T DEVELOP, FORTUNATELY!
HEY THERE, SMARTY-PANTS, WHAT ARE YOU DOING OVER MY WASH?
WASH?!
OH, NO!
KROTOS *ADORE* SOAP!
OH, GOOD JOB! WELL DONE!

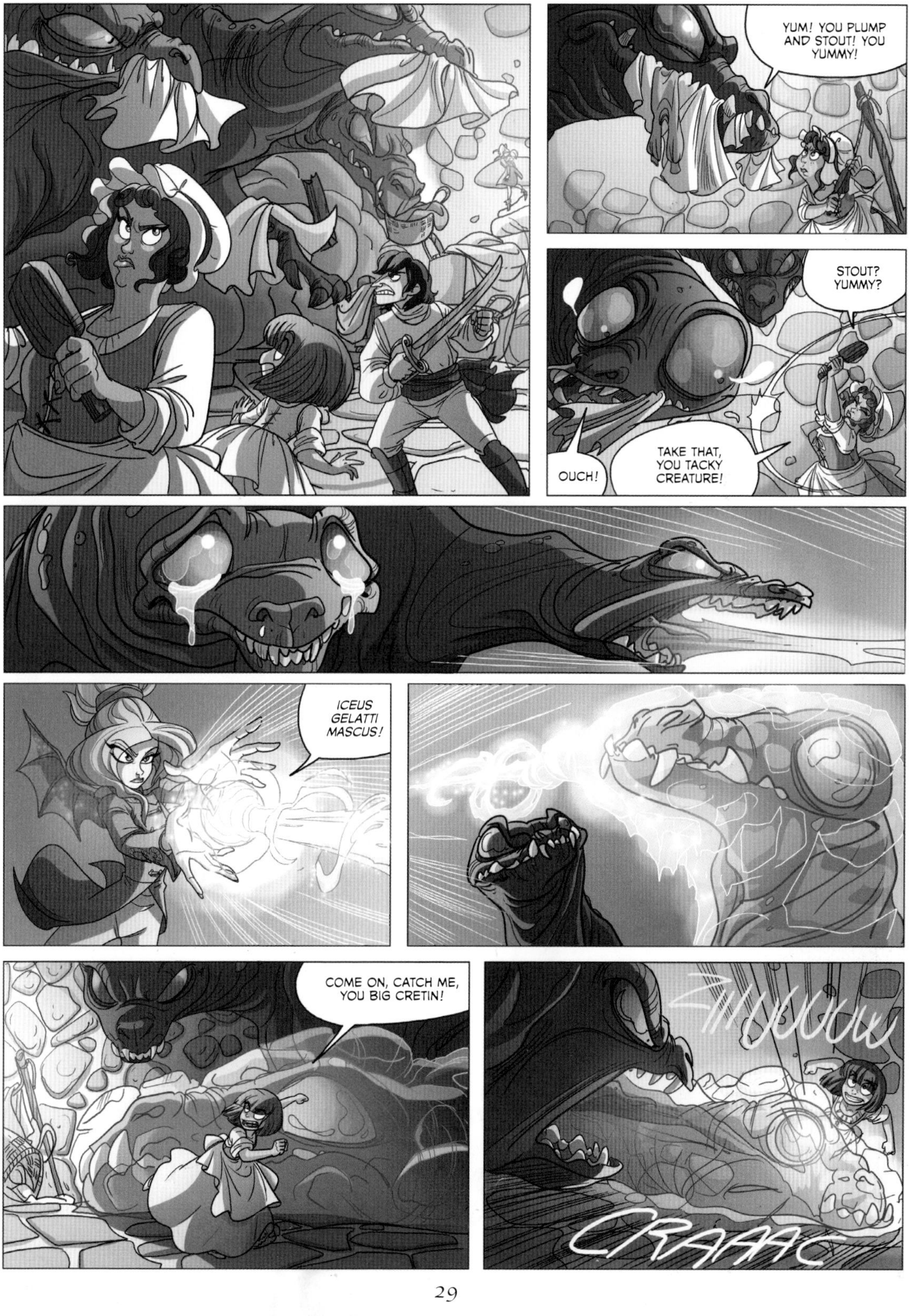

YUM! YOU PLUMP AND STOUT! YOU YUMMY!
STOUT? YUMMY?
TAKE THAT, YOU TACKY CREATURE!
OUCH!
ICEUS GELATTI MASCUS!
COME ON, CATCH ME, YOU BIG CRETIN!
ZIIIUUUUUW
CRAAAC

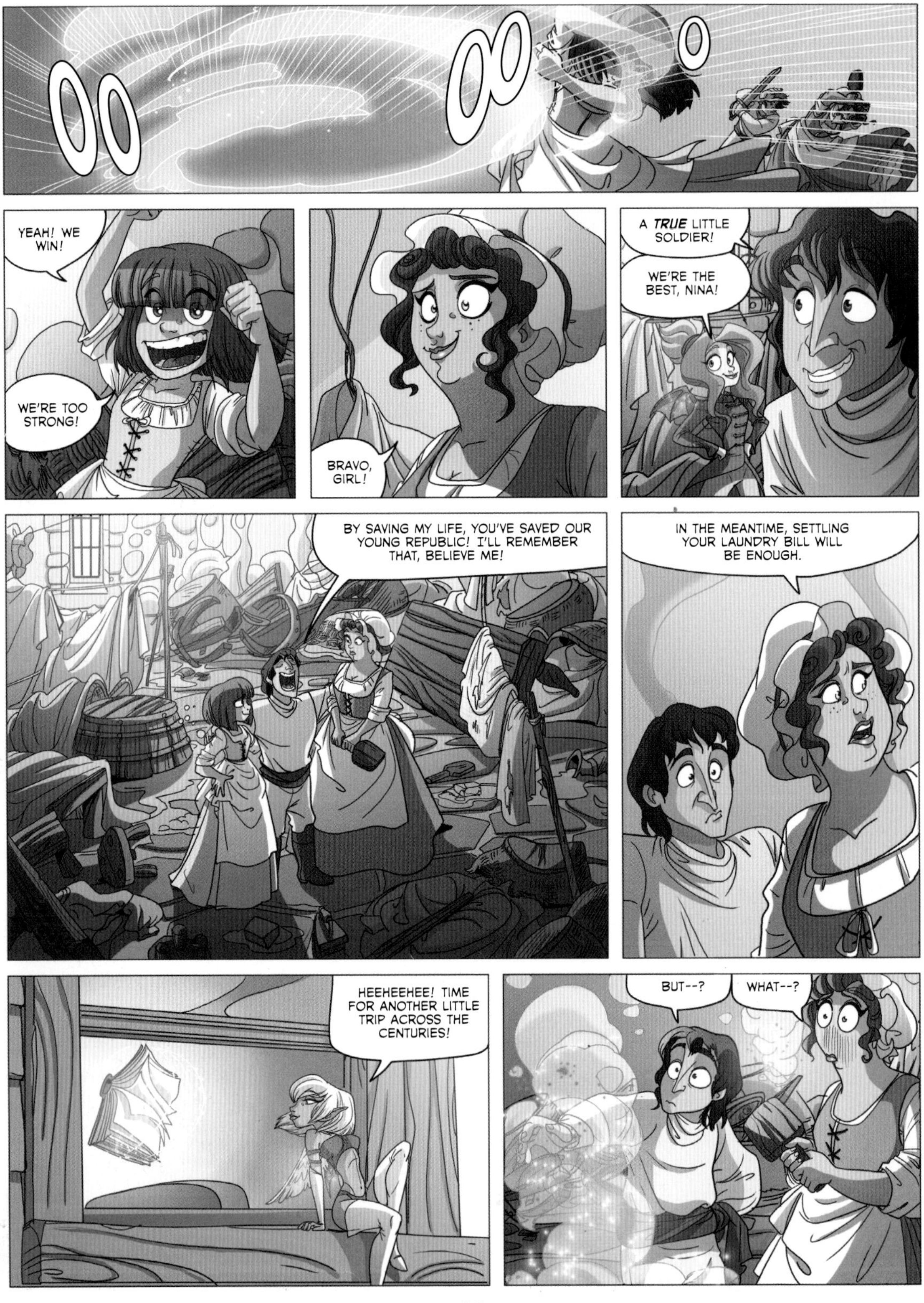
OO
OO
O
YEAH! WE WIN!
WE'RE TOO STRONG!
BRAVO, GIRL!
A TRUE LITTLE SOLDIER!
WE'RE THE BEST, NINA!
BY SAVING MY LIFE, YOU'VE SAVED OUR YOUNG REPUBLIC! I'LL REMEMBER THAT, BELIEVE ME!
IN THE MEANTIME, SETTLING YOUR LAUNDRY BILL WILL BE ENOUGH.
HEEHEEHEE! TIME FOR ANOTHER LITTLE TRIP ACROSS THE CENTURIES!
BUT--?
WHAT--?

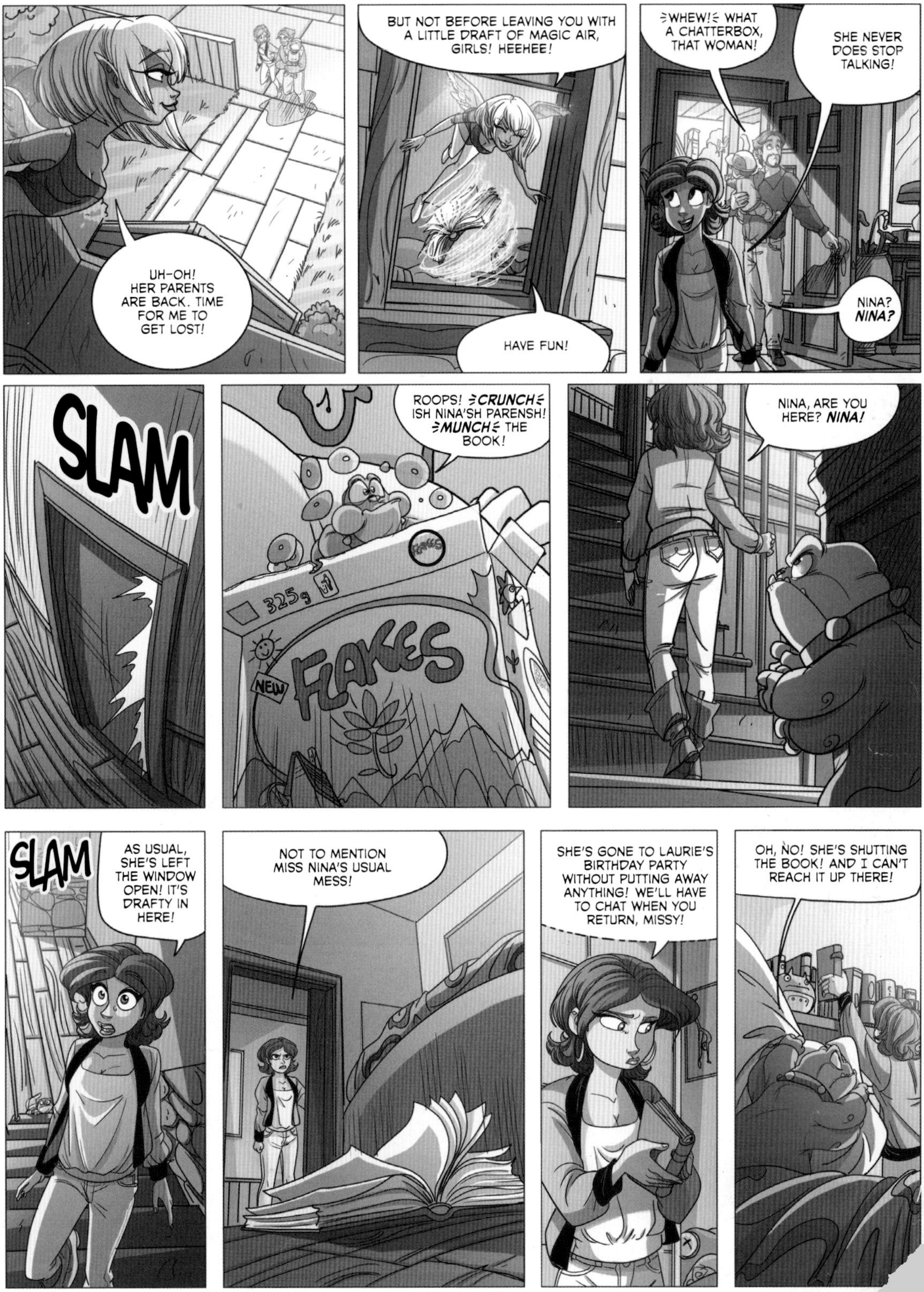
UH-OH! HER PARENTS ARE BACK. TIME FOR ME TO GET LOST!
BUT NOT BEFORE LEAVING YOU WITH A LITTLE DRAFT OF MAGIC AIR, GIRLS! HEEHEE!
HAVE FUN!
WHEW! WHAT A CHATTERBOX, THAT WOMAN!
SHE NEVER DOES STOP TALKING!
NINA? NINA?
SLAM
ROOPS! CRUNCH ISH NINA'SH PARENSH! MUNCH THE BOOK!
FLAKES
325g
NEW
FLAKES
NINA, ARE YOU HERE? NINA!
SLAM
AS USUAL, SHE'S LEFT THE WINDOW OPEN! IT'S DRAFTY IN HERE!
NOT TO MENTION MISS NINA'S USUAL MESS!
SHE'S GONE TO LAURIE'S BIRTHDAY PARTY WITHOUT PUTTING AWAY ANYTHING! WE'LL HAVE TO CHAT WHEN YOU RETURN, MISSY!
OH, NO! SHE'S SHUTTING THE BOOK! AND I CAN'T REACH IT UP THERE!

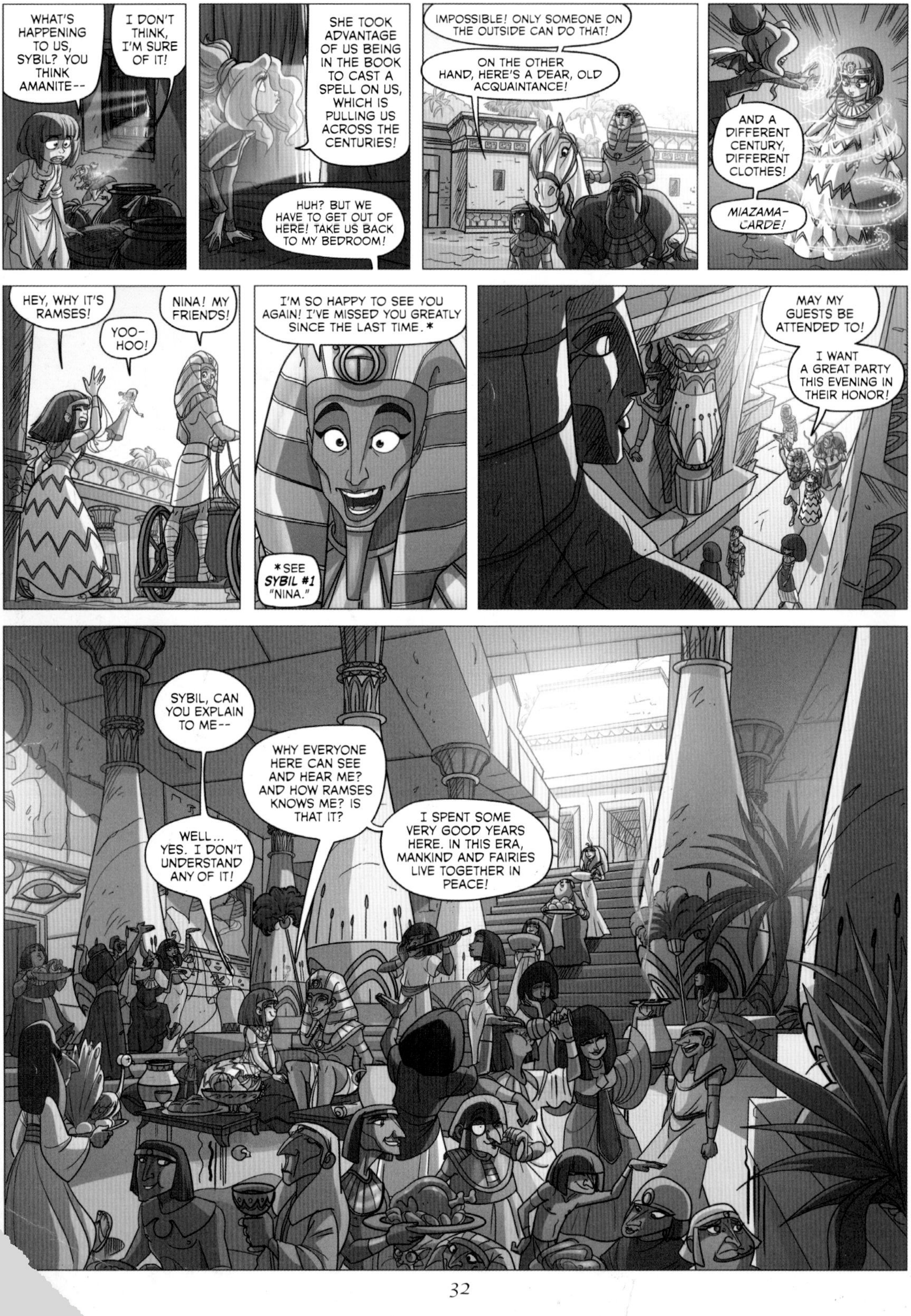
WHAT'S HAPPENING TO US, SYBIL? YOU THINK AMANITE--
I DON'T THINK, I'M SURE OF IT!
SHE TOOK ADVANTAGE OF US BEING IN THE BOOK TO CAST A SPELL ON US, WHICH IS PULLING US ACROSS THE CENTURIES!
HUH? BUT WE HAVE TO GET OUT OF HERE! TAKE US BACK TO MY BEDROOM!
IMPOSSIBLE! ONLY SOMEONE ON THE OUTSIDE CAN DO THAT!
ON THE OTHER HAND, HERE'S A DEAR, OLD ACQUAINTANCE!
AND A DIFFERENT CENTURY, DIFFERENT CLOTHES!
MIAZAMA-CARDE!
HEY, WHY IT'S RAMSES!
YOO-HOO!
NINA! MY FRIENDS!
I'M SO HAPPY TO SEE YOU AGAIN! I'VE MISSED YOU GREATLY SINCE THE LAST TIME.*
*SEE SYBIL #1 "NINA."
MAY MY GUESTS BE ATTENDED TO!
I WANT A GREAT PARTY THIS EVENING IN THEIR HONOR!
SYBIL, CAN YOU EXPLAIN TO ME--
WHY EVERYONE HERE CAN SEE AND HEAR ME? AND HOW RAMSES KNOWS ME? IS THAT IT?
WELL... YES. I DON'T UNDERSTAND ANY OF IT!
I SPENT SOME VERY GOOD YEARS HERE. IN THIS ERA, MANKIND AND FAIRIES LIVE TOGETHER IN PEACE!

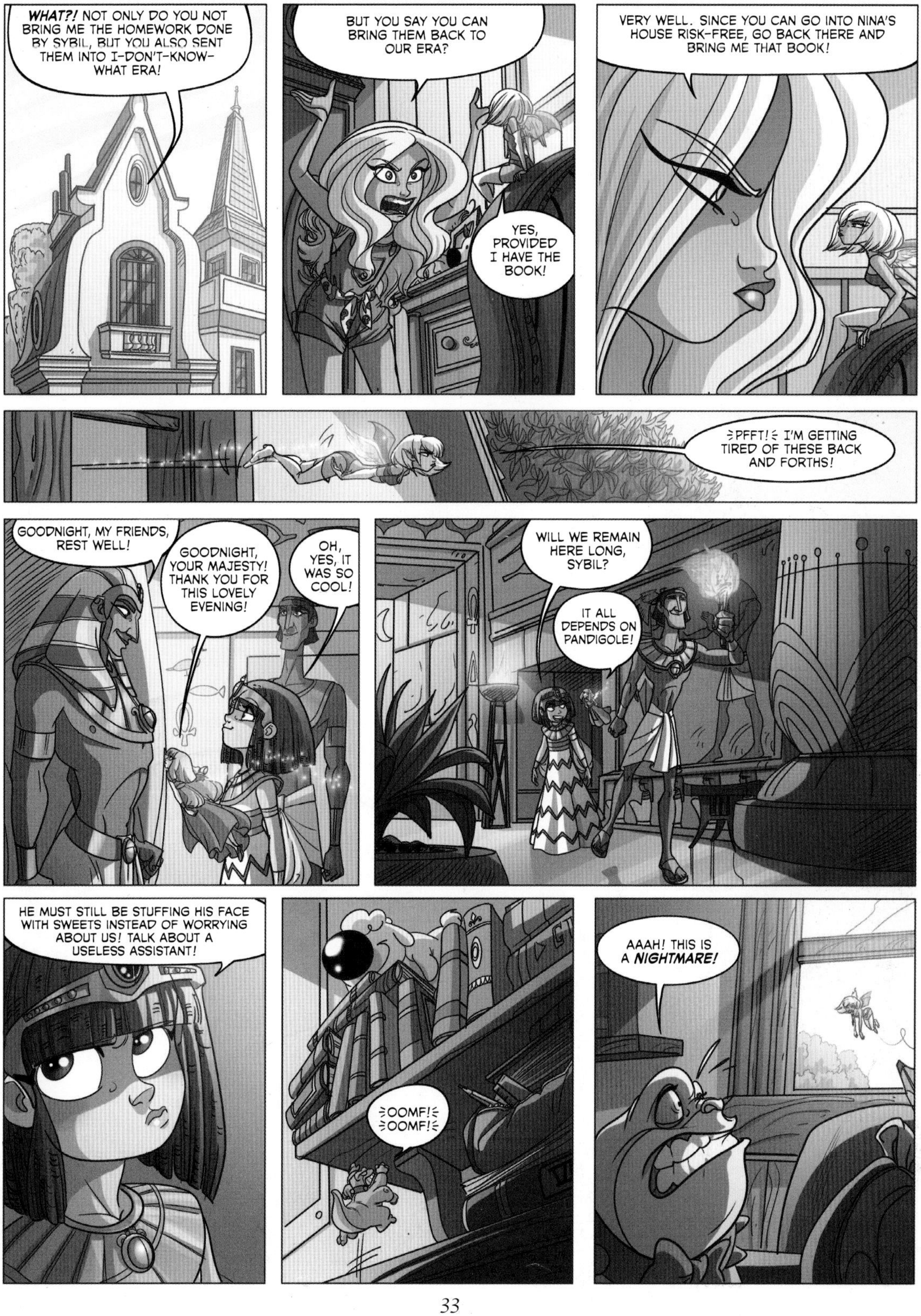
WHAT?! NOT ONLY DO YOU NOT BRING ME THE HOMEWORK DONE BY SYBIL, BUT YOU ALSO SENT THEM INTO I-DON'T-KNOW-WHAT ERA!
BUT YOU SAY YOU CAN BRING THEM BACK TO OUR ERA?
YES, PROVIDED I HAVE THE BOOK!
VERY WELL. SINCE YOU CAN GO INTO NINA'S HOUSE RISK-FREE, GO BACK THERE AND BRING ME THAT BOOK!
PFFT! I'M GETTING TIRED OF THESE BACK AND FORTHS!
GOODNIGHT, MY FRIENDS, REST WELL!
GOODNIGHT, YOUR MAJESTY! THANK YOU FOR THIS LOVELY EVENING!
OH, YES, IT WAS SO COOL!
WILL WE REMAIN HERE LONG, SYBIL?
IT ALL DEPENDS ON PANDIGOLE!
HE MUST STILL BE STUFFING HIS FACE WITH SWEETS INSTEAD OF WORRYING ABOUT US! TALK ABOUT A USELESS ASSISTANT!
OOMF! OOMF!
AAAH! THIS IS A NIGHTMARE!

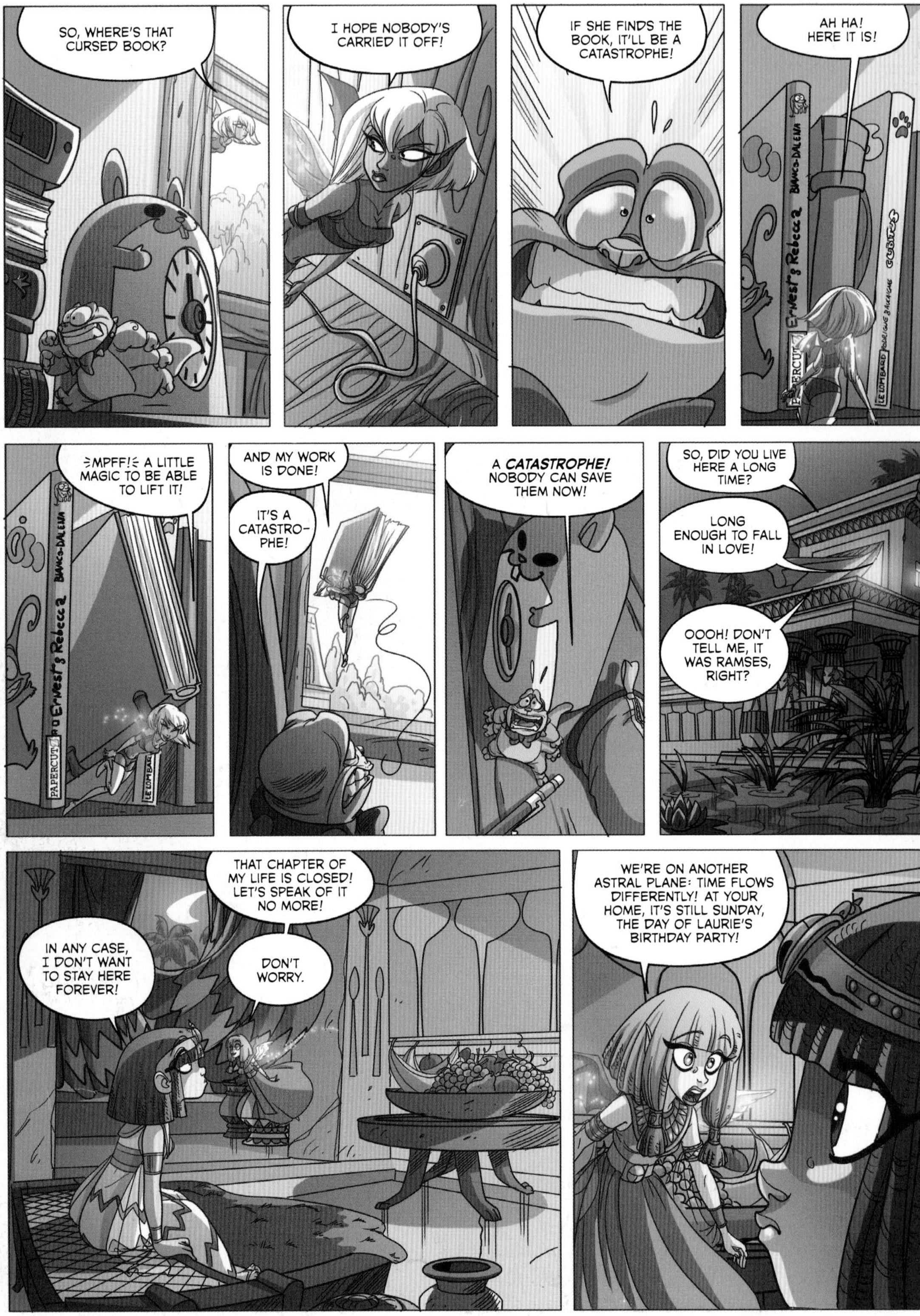
SO, WHERE'S THAT CURSED BOOK?
I HOPE NOBODY'S CARRIED IT OFF!
IF SHE FINDS THE BOOK, IT'LL BE A CATASTROPHE!
AH HA! HERE IT IS!
≶MPFF!≶ A LITTLE MAGIC TO BE ABLE TO LIFT IT!
AND MY WORK IS DONE!
IT'S A CATASTROPHE!
A *CATASTROPHE!* NOBODY CAN SAVE THEM NOW!
SO, DID YOU LIVE HERE A LONG TIME?
LONG ENOUGH TO FALL IN LOVE!
OOOH! DON'T TELL ME, IT WAS RAMSES, RIGHT?
THAT CHAPTER OF MY LIFE IS CLOSED! LET'S SPEAK OF IT NO MORE!
IN ANY CASE, I DON'T WANT TO STAY HERE FOREVER!
DON'T WORRY.
WE'RE ON ANOTHER ASTRAL PLANE: TIME FLOWS DIFFERENTLY! AT YOUR HOME, IT'S STILL SUNDAY, THE DAY OF LAURIE'S BIRTHDAY PARTY!

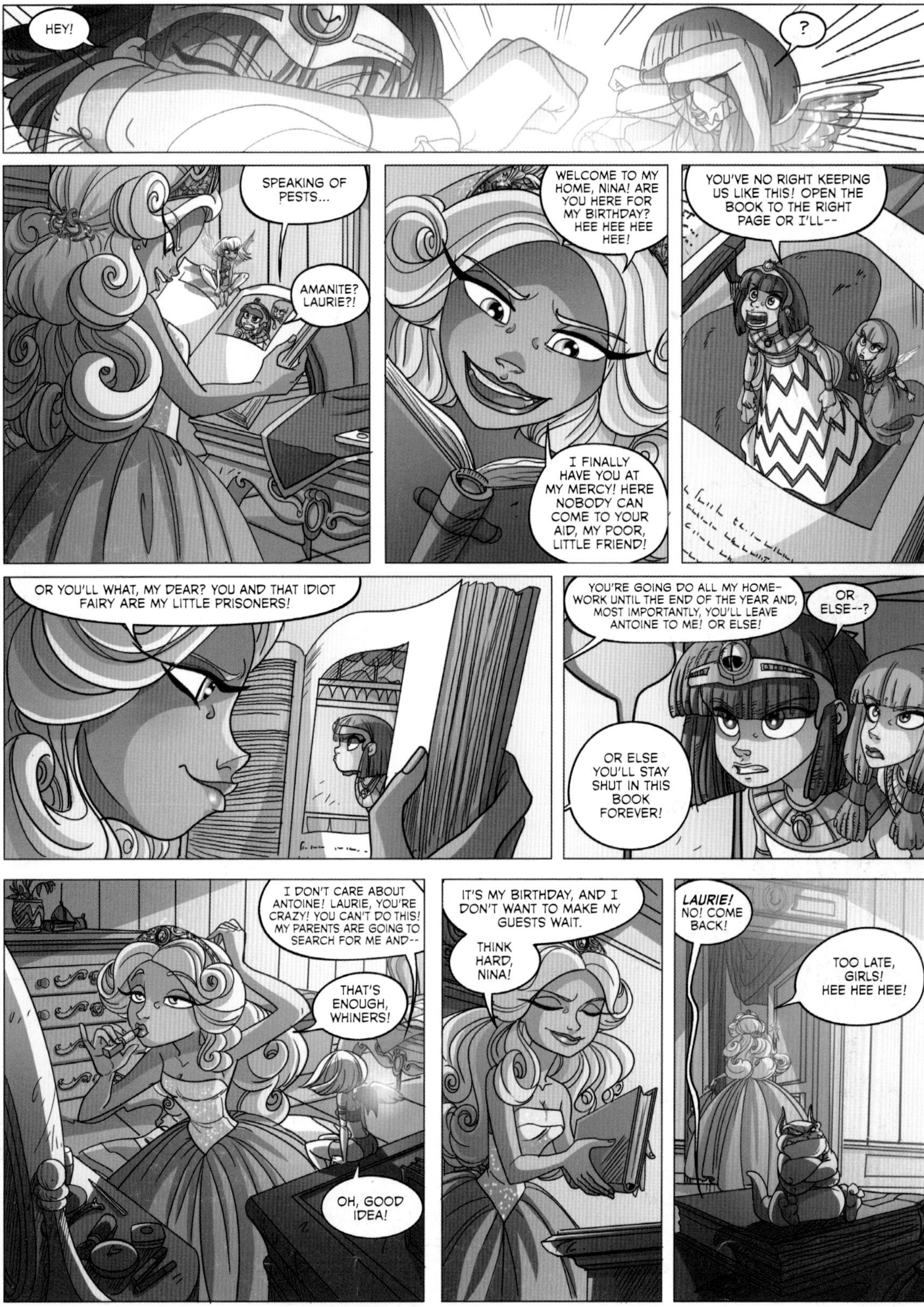
HEY!
?
SPEAKING OF PESTS...
AMANITE? LAURIE?!
WELCOME TO MY HOME, NINA! ARE YOU HERE FOR MY BIRTHDAY? HEE HEE HEE HEE!
I FINALLY HAVE YOU AT MY MERCY! HERE NOBODY CAN COME TO YOUR AID, MY POOR, LITTLE FRIEND!
YOU'VE NO RIGHT KEEPING US LIKE THIS! OPEN THE BOOK TO THE RIGHT PAGE OR I'LL--
OR YOU'LL WHAT, MY DEAR? YOU AND THAT IDIOT FAIRY ARE MY LITTLE PRISONERS!
YOU'RE GOING DO ALL MY HOME-WORK UNTIL THE END OF THE YEAR AND, MOST IMPORTANTLY, YOU'LL LEAVE ANTOINE TO ME! OR ELSE!
OR ELSE--?
OR ELSE YOU'LL STAY SHUT IN THIS BOOK FOREVER!
I DON'T CARE ABOUT ANTOINE! LAURIE, YOU'RE CRAZY! YOU CAN'T DO THIS! MY PARENTS ARE GOING TO SEARCH FOR ME AND--
THAT'S ENOUGH, WHINERS!
OH, GOOD IDEA!
IT'S MY BIRTHDAY, AND I DON'T WANT TO MAKE MY GUESTS WAIT.
THINK HARD, NINA!
LAURIE! NO! COME BACK!
TOO LATE, GIRLS! HEE HEE HEE!

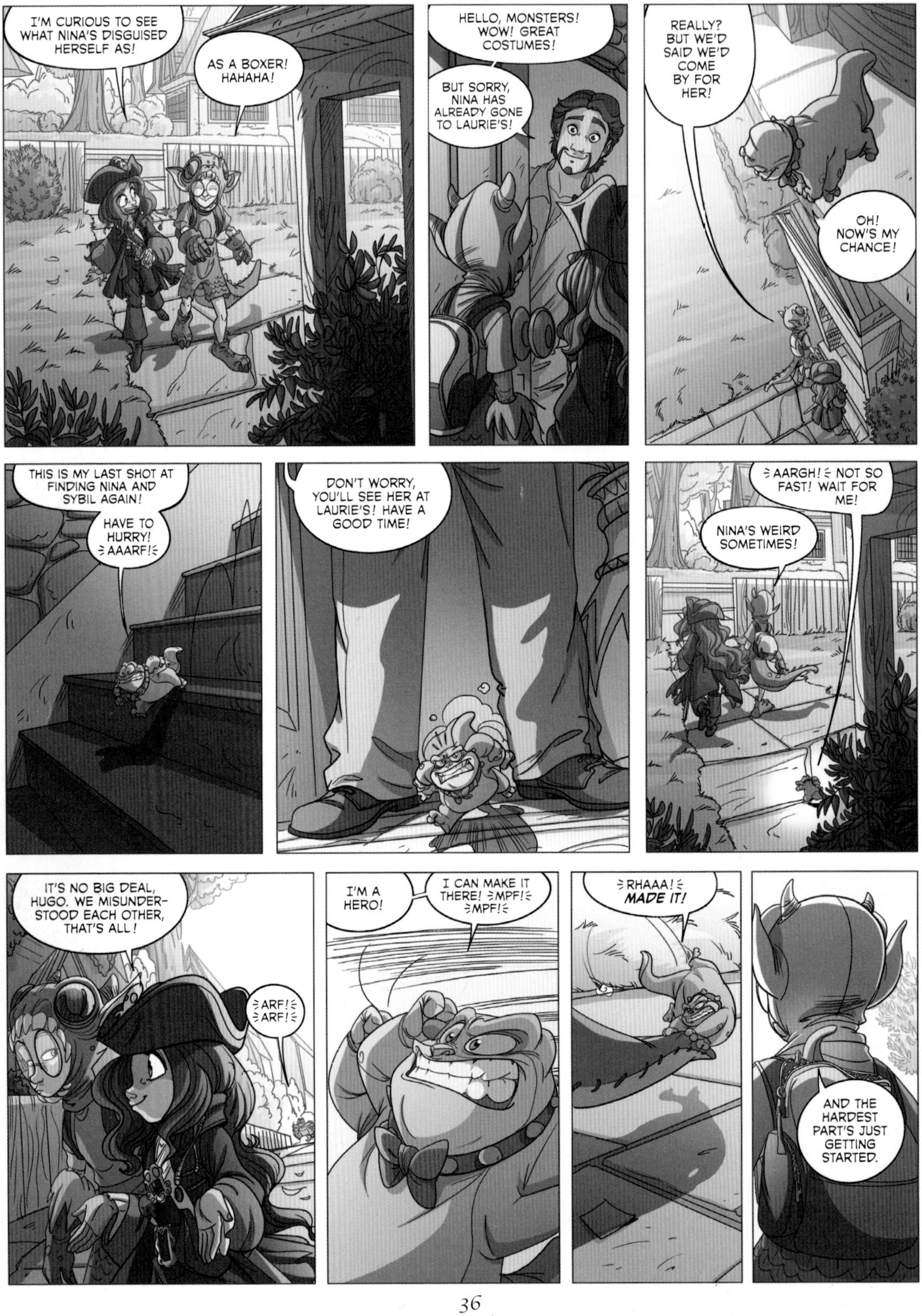

I'M CURIOUS TO SEE WHAT NINA'S DISGUISED HERSELF AS!
AS A BOXER! HAHAHA!
HELLO, MONSTERS! WOW! GREAT COSTUMES!
BUT SORRY, NINA HAS ALREADY GONE TO LAURIE'S!
REALLY? BUT WE'D SAID WE'D COME BY FOR HER!
OH! NOW'S MY CHANCE!
THIS IS MY LAST SHOT AT FINDING NINA AND SYBIL AGAIN!
HAVE TO HURRY! AAARF!
DON'T WORRY, YOU'LL SEE HER AT LAURIE'S! HAVE A GOOD TIME!
AARGH! NOT SO FAST! WAIT FOR ME!
NINA'S WEIRD SOMETIMES!
IT'S NO BIG DEAL, HUGO. WE MISUNDER-STOOD EACH OTHER, THAT'S ALL!
ARF! ARF!
I'M A HERO!
I CAN MAKE IT THERE! MPF! MPF!
RHAAA! *MADE IT!*
AND THE HARDEST PART'S JUST GETTING STARTED.

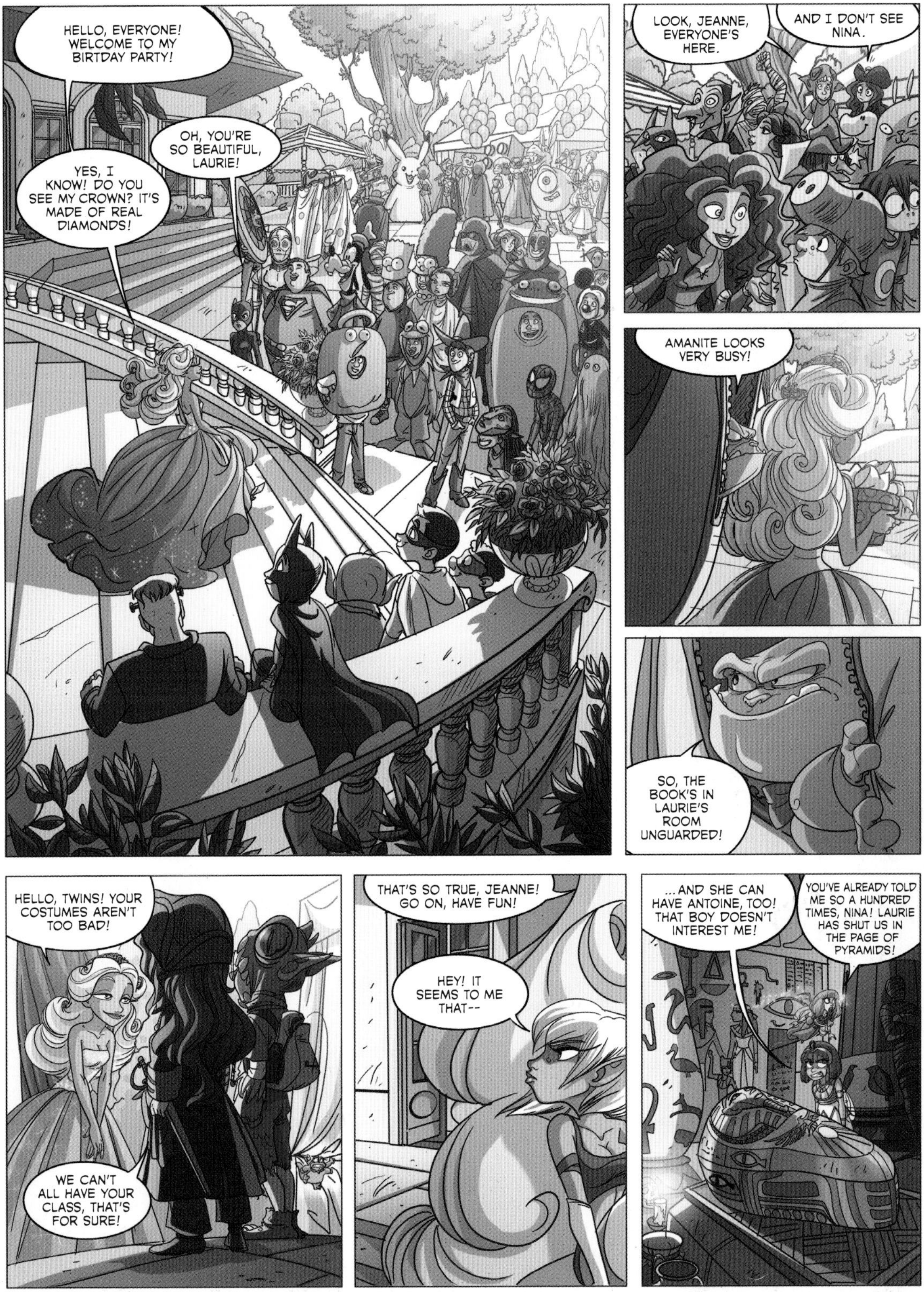
HELLO, EVERYONE! WELCOME TO MY BIRTDAY PARTY!
OH, YOU'RE SO BEAUTIFUL, LAURIE!
YES, I KNOW! DO YOU SEE MY CROWN? IT'S MADE OF REAL DIAMONDS!
LOOK, JEANNE, EVERYONE'S HERE.
AND I DON'T SEE NINA.
AMANITE LOOKS VERY BUSY!
SO, THE BOOK'S IN LAURIE'S ROOM UNGUARDED!
HELLO, TWINS! YOUR COSTUMES AREN'T TOO BAD!
WE CAN'T ALL HAVE YOUR CLASS, THAT'S FOR SURE!
THAT'S SO TRUE, JEANNE! GO ON, HAVE FUN!
HEY! IT SEEMS TO ME THAT--
...AND SHE CAN HAVE ANTOINE, TOO! THAT BOY DOESN'T INTEREST ME!
YOU'VE ALREADY TOLD ME SO A HUNDRED TIMES, NINA! LAURIE HAS SHUT US IN THE PAGE OF PYRAMIDS!

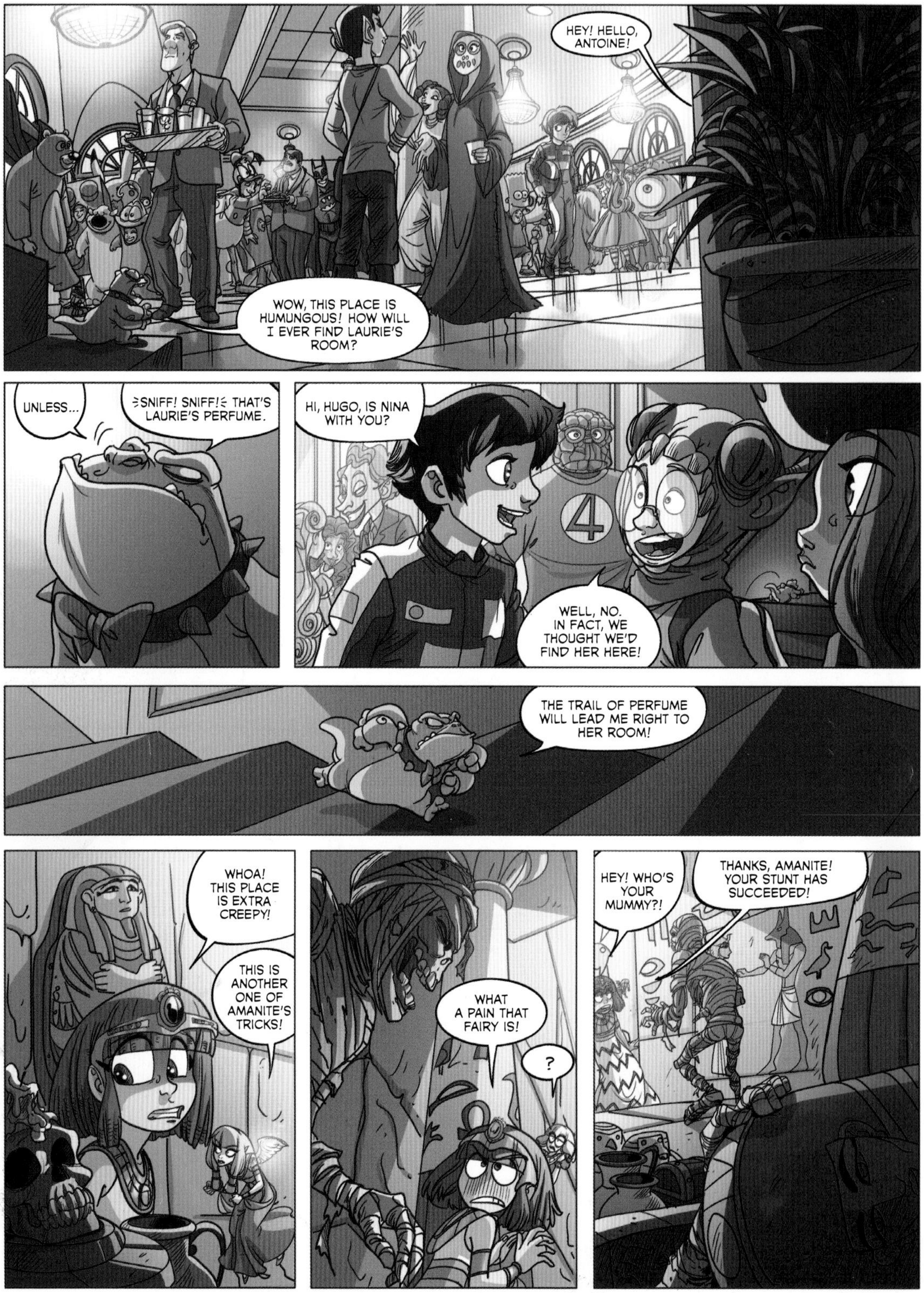
HEY! HELLO, ANTOINE!
WOW, THIS PLACE IS HUMUNGOUS! HOW WILL I EVER FIND LAURIE'S ROOM?
UNLESS...
SNIFF! SNIFF! THAT'S LAURIE'S PERFUME.
HI, HUGO, IS NINA WITH YOU?
WELL, NO. IN FACT, WE THOUGHT WE'D FIND HER HERE!
THE TRAIL OF PERFUME WILL LEAD ME RIGHT TO HER ROOM!
WHOA! THIS PLACE IS EXTRA CREEPY!
THIS IS ANOTHER ONE OF AMANITE'S TRICKS!
WHAT A PAIN THAT FAIRY IS!
?
HEY! WHO'S YOUR MUMMY?!
THANKS, AMANITE! YOUR STUNT HAS SUCCEEDED!
4

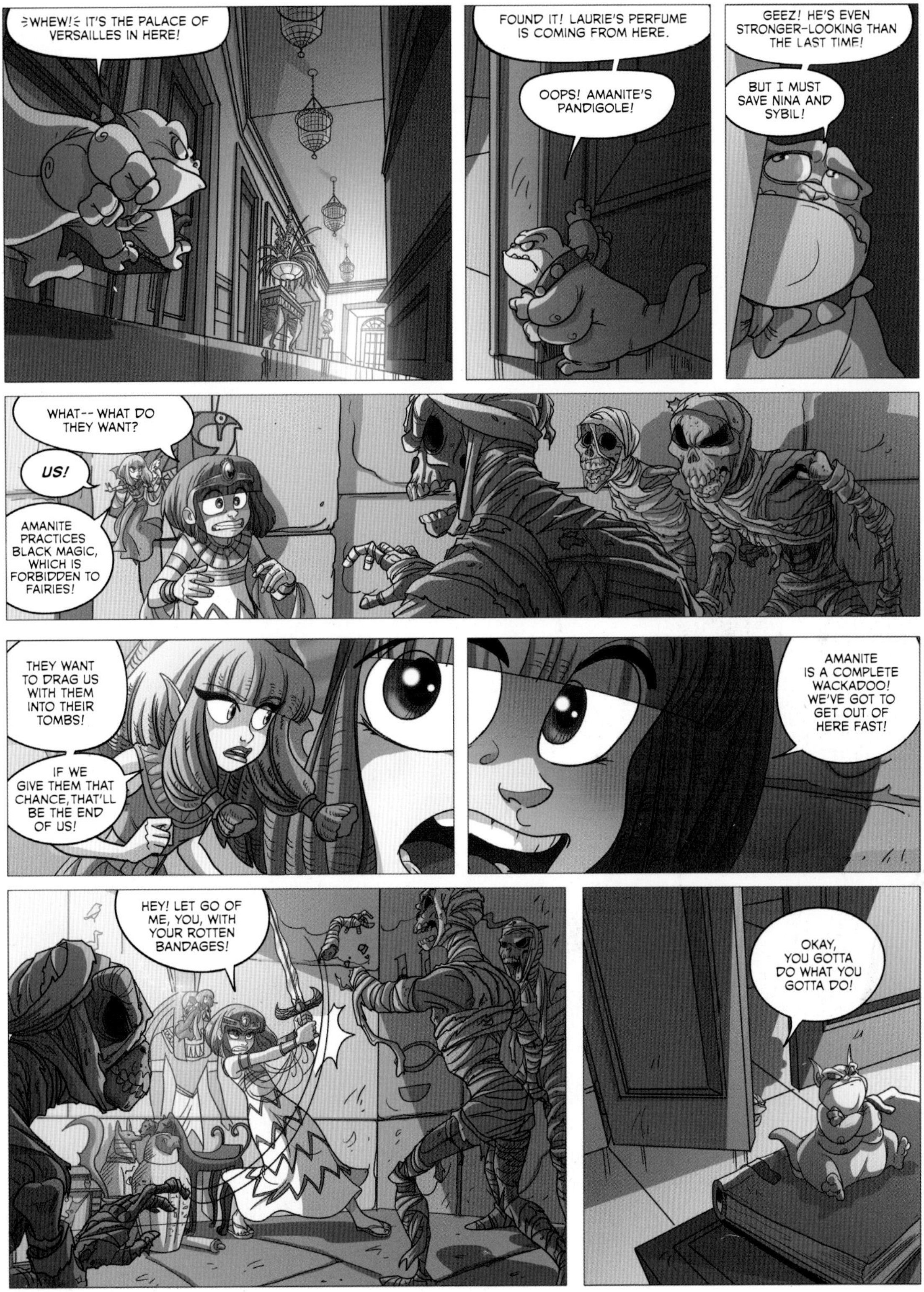

≶WHEW!≷ IT'S THE PALACE OF VERSAILLES IN HERE!
FOUND IT! LAURIE'S PERFUME IS COMING FROM HERE.
OOPS! AMANITE'S PANDIGOLE!
GEEZ! HE'S EVEN STRONGER-LOOKING THAN THE LAST TIME!
BUT I MUST SAVE NINA AND SYBIL!
WHAT-- WHAT DO THEY WANT?
US!
AMANITE PRACTICES BLACK MAGIC, WHICH IS FORBIDDEN TO FAIRIES!
THEY WANT TO DRAG US WITH THEM INTO THEIR TOMBS!
IF WE GIVE THEM THAT CHANCE, THAT'LL BE THE END OF US!
AMANITE IS A COMPLETE WACKADOO! WE'VE GOT TO GET OUT OF HERE FAST!
HEY! LET GO OF ME, YOU, WITH YOUR ROTTEN BANDAGES!
OKAY, YOU GOTTA DO WHAT YOU GOTTA DO!

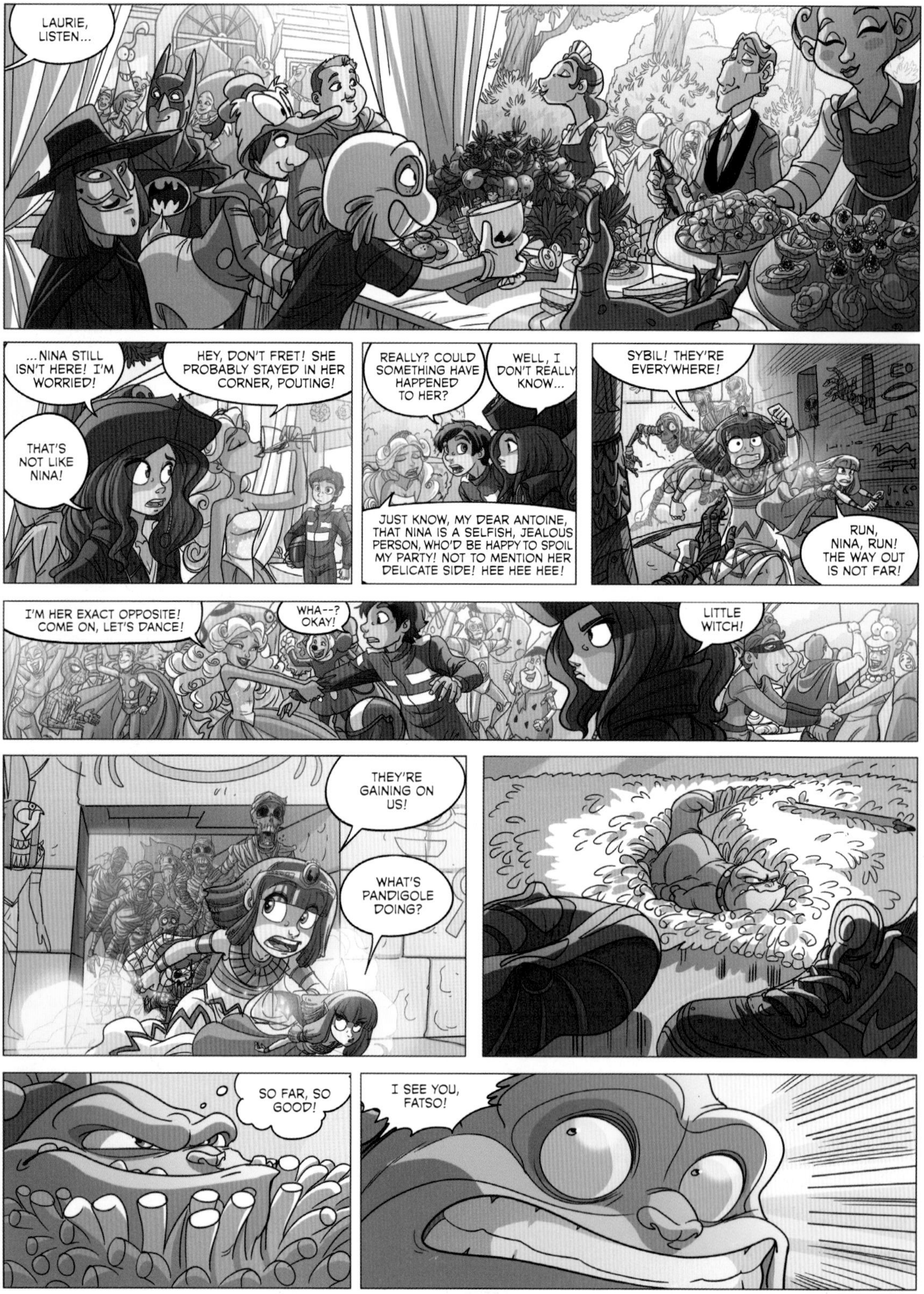
LAURIE, LISTEN...
...NINA STILL ISN'T HERE! I'M WORRIED!
HEY, DON'T FRET! SHE PROBABLY STAYED IN HER CORNER, POUTING!
THAT'S NOT LIKE NINA!
REALLY? COULD SOMETHING HAVE HAPPENED TO HER?
WELL, I DON'T REALLY KNOW...
JUST KNOW, MY DEAR ANTOINE, THAT NINA IS A SELFISH, JEALOUS PERSON, WHO'D BE HAPPY TO SPOIL MY PARTY! NOT TO MENTION HER DELICATE SIDE! HEE HEE HEE!
SYBIL! THEY'RE EVERYWHERE!
RUN, NINA, RUN! THE WAY OUT IS NOT FAR!
I'M HER EXACT OPPOSITE! COME ON, LET'S DANCE!
WHA--? OKAY!
LITTLE WITCH!
THEY'RE GAINING ON US!
WHAT'S PANDIGOLE DOING?
SO FAR, SO GOOD!
I SEE YOU, FATSO!

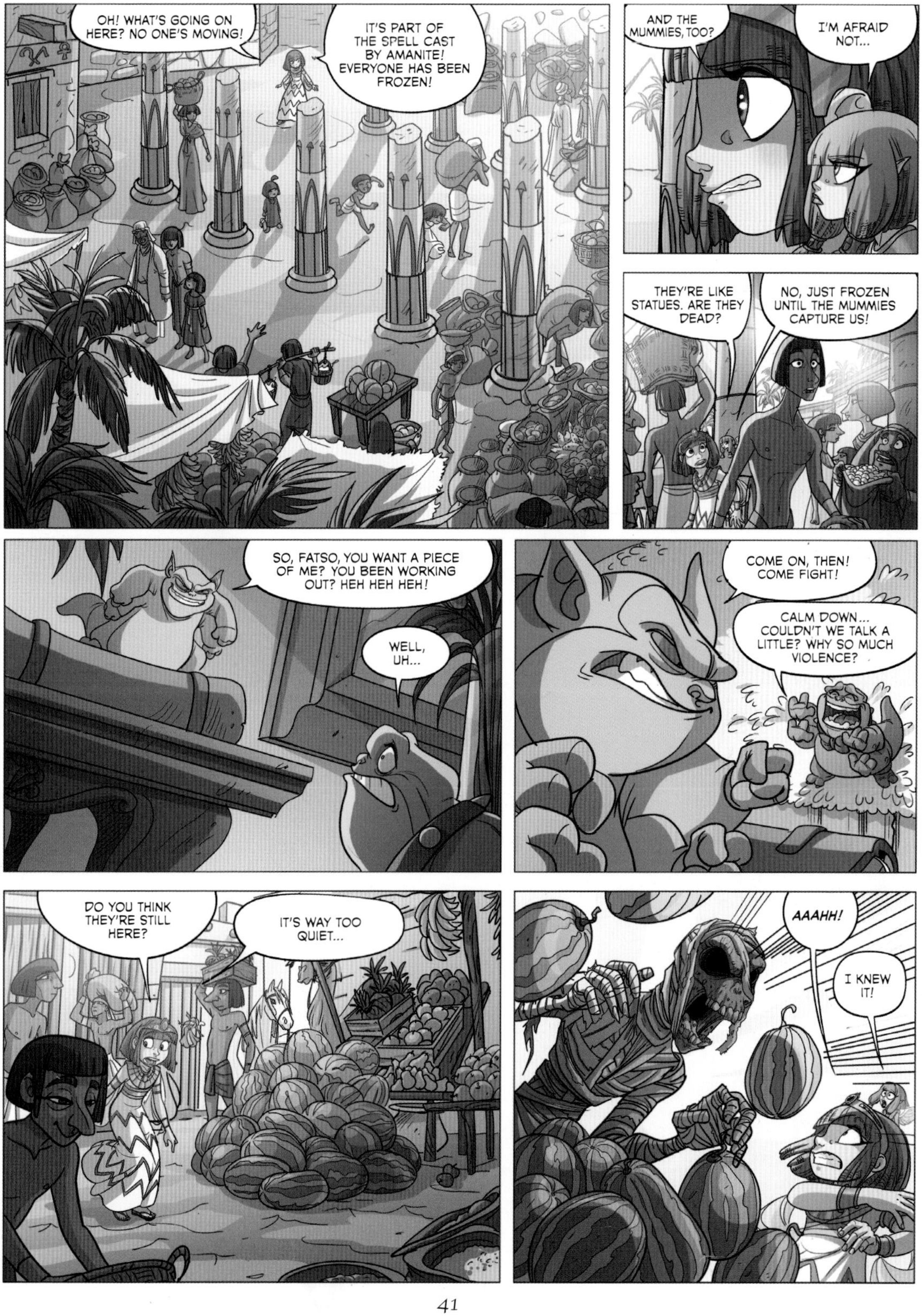
OH! WHAT'S GOING ON HERE? NO ONE'S MOVING!
IT'S PART OF THE SPELL CAST BY AMANITE! EVERYONE HAS BEEN FROZEN!
AND THE MUMMIES, TOO?
I'M AFRAID NOT...
THEY'RE LIKE STATUES. ARE THEY DEAD?
NO, JUST FROZEN UNTIL THE MUMMIES CAPTURE US!
SO, FATSO, YOU WANT A PIECE OF ME? YOU BEEN WORKING OUT? HEH HEH HEH!
WELL, UH...
COME ON, THEN! COME FIGHT!
CALM DOWN... COULDN'T WE TALK A LITTLE? WHY SO MUCH VIOLENCE?
DO YOU THINK THEY'RE STILL HERE?
IT'S WAY TOO QUIET...
AAAHH!
I KNEW IT!

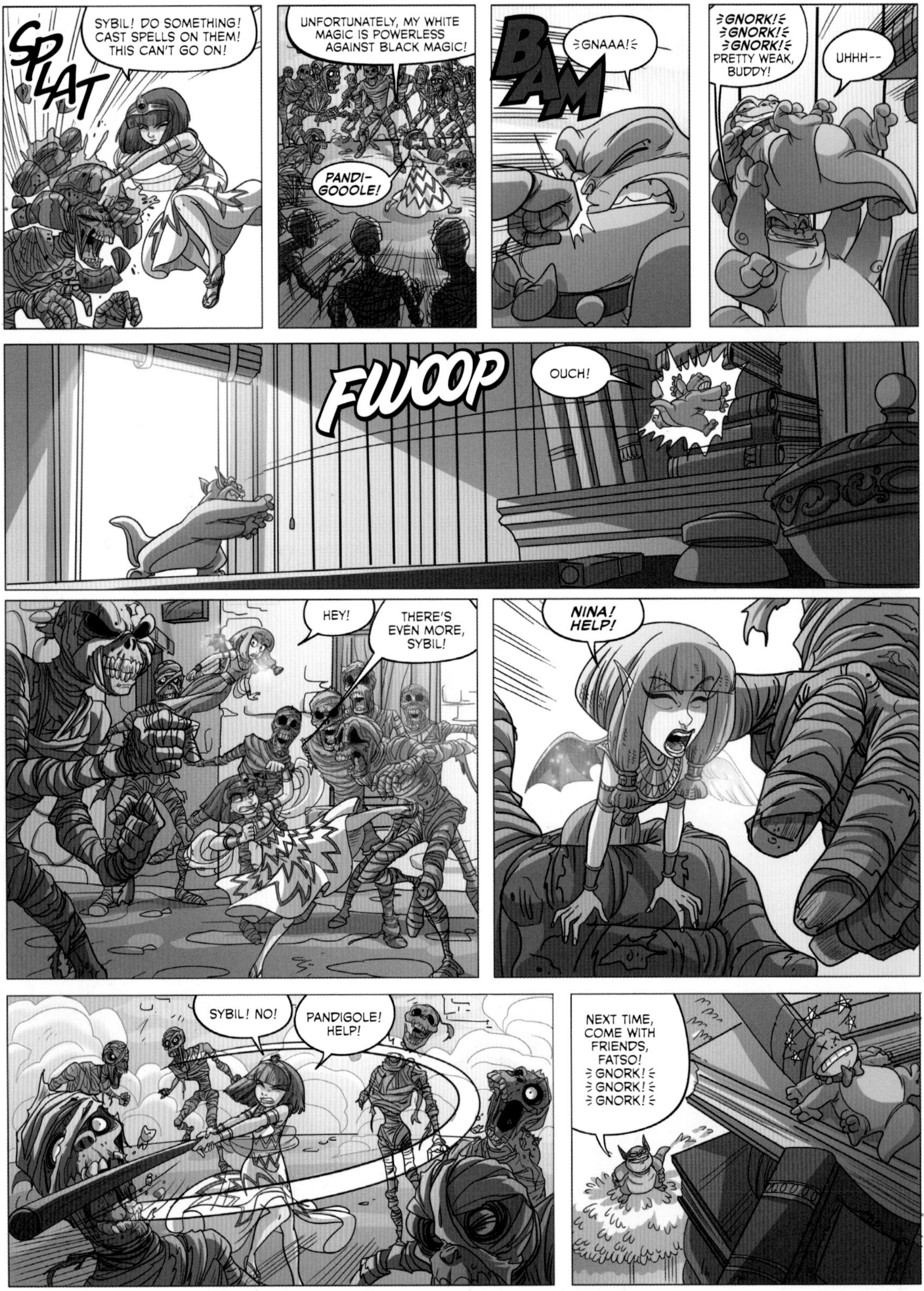
SPLAT
SYBIL! DO SOMETHING! CAST SPELLS ON THEM! THIS CAN'T GO ON!
UNFORTUNATELY, MY WHITE MAGIC IS POWERLESS AGAINST BLACK MAGIC!
PANDI-GOOOLE!
BAM
GNAAA!
GNORK! GNORK! GNORK! PRETTY WEAK, BUDDY!
UHHH--
FWOOP
OUCH!
HEY!
THERE'S EVEN MORE, SYBIL!
NINA! HELP!
SYBIL! NO!
PANDIGOLE! HELP!
NEXT TIME, COME WITH FRIENDS, FATSO! GNORK! GNORK! GNORK!

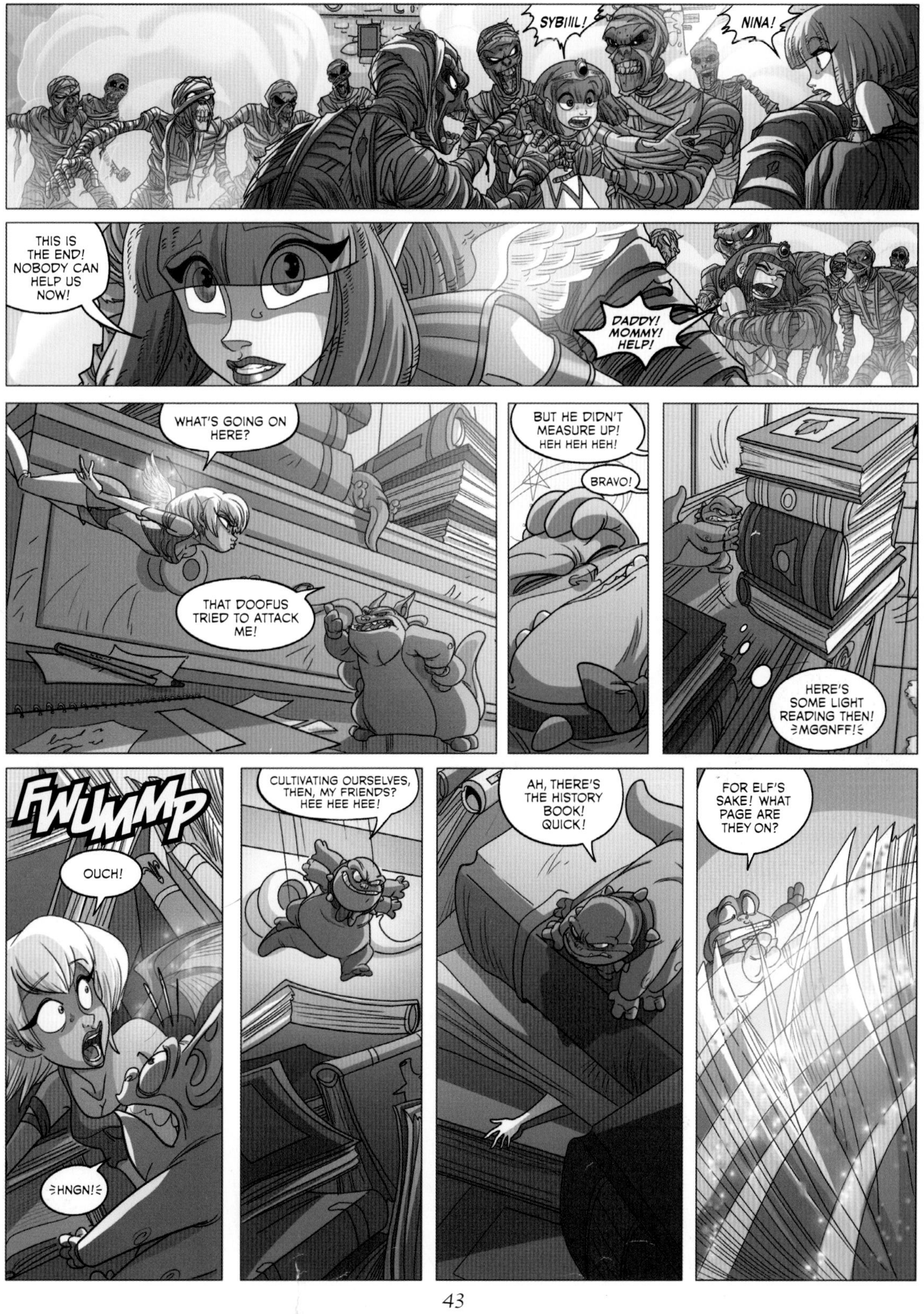
SYBIIIL!
NINA!
THIS IS THE END! NOBODY CAN HELP US NOW!
DADDY! MOMMY! HELP!
WHAT'S GOING ON HERE?
THAT DOOFUS TRIED TO ATTACK ME!
BUT HE DIDN'T MEASURE UP! HEH HEH HEH!
BRAVO!
HERE'S SOME LIGHT READING THEN! MGGNFF!
FWUMMP
OUCH!
HNGN!
CULTIVATING OURSELVES, THEN, MY FRIENDS? HEE HEE HEE!
AH, THERE'S THE HISTORY BOOK! QUICK!
FOR ELF'S SAKE! WHAT PAGE ARE THEY ON?

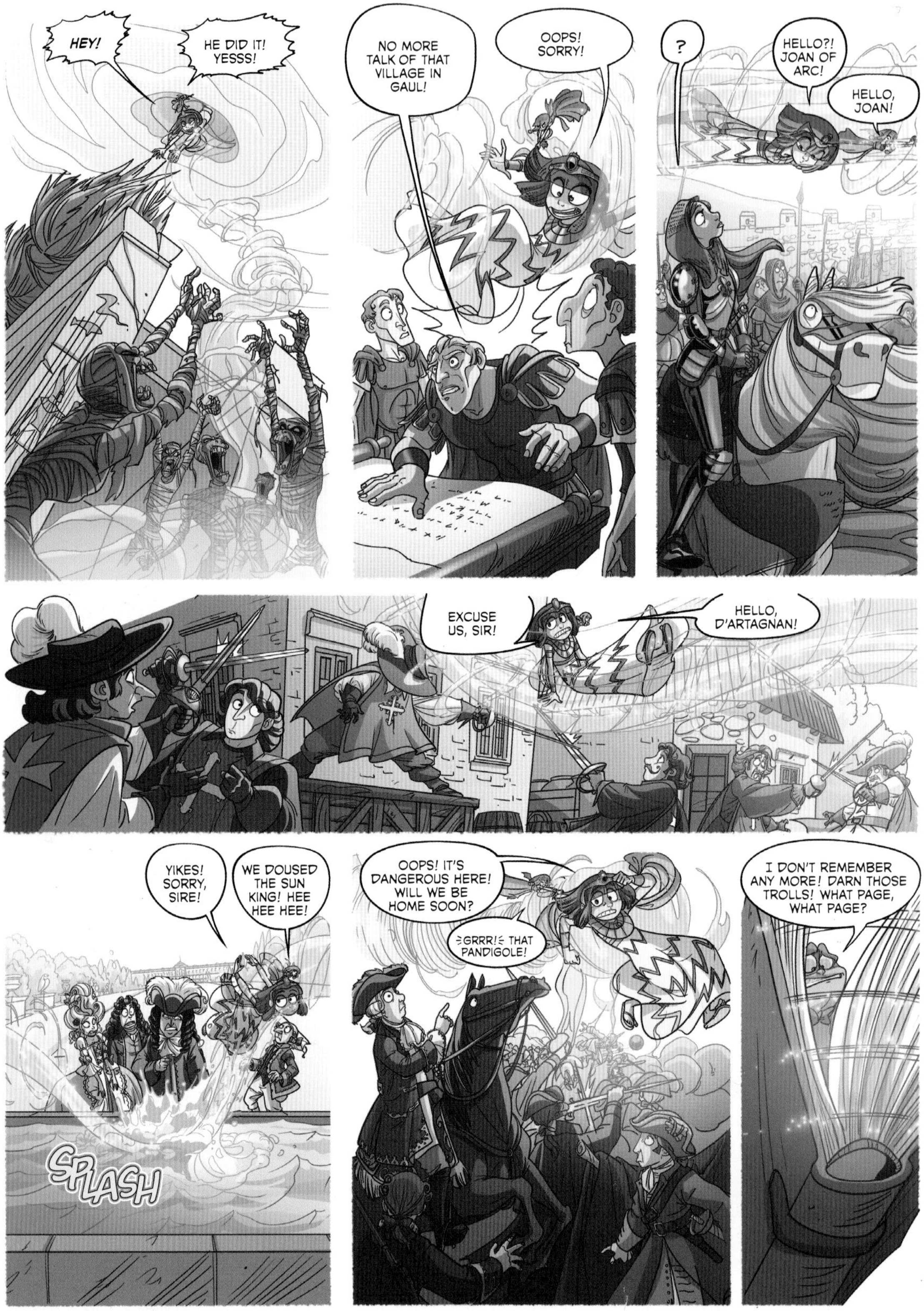
HEY!
HE DID IT! YESSS!
NO MORE TALK OF THAT VILLAGE IN GAUL!
OOPS! SORRY!
?
HELLO?! JOAN OF ARC!
HELLO, JOAN!
EXCUSE US, SIR!
HELLO, D'ARTAGNAN!
YIKES! SORRY, SIRE!
WE DOUSED THE SUN KING! HEE HEE HEE!
SPLASH
OOPS! IT'S DANGEROUS HERE! WILL WE BE HOME SOON?
GRRR! THAT PANDIGOLE!
I DON'T REMEMBER ANY MORE! DARN THOSE TROLLS! WHAT PAGE, WHAT PAGE?

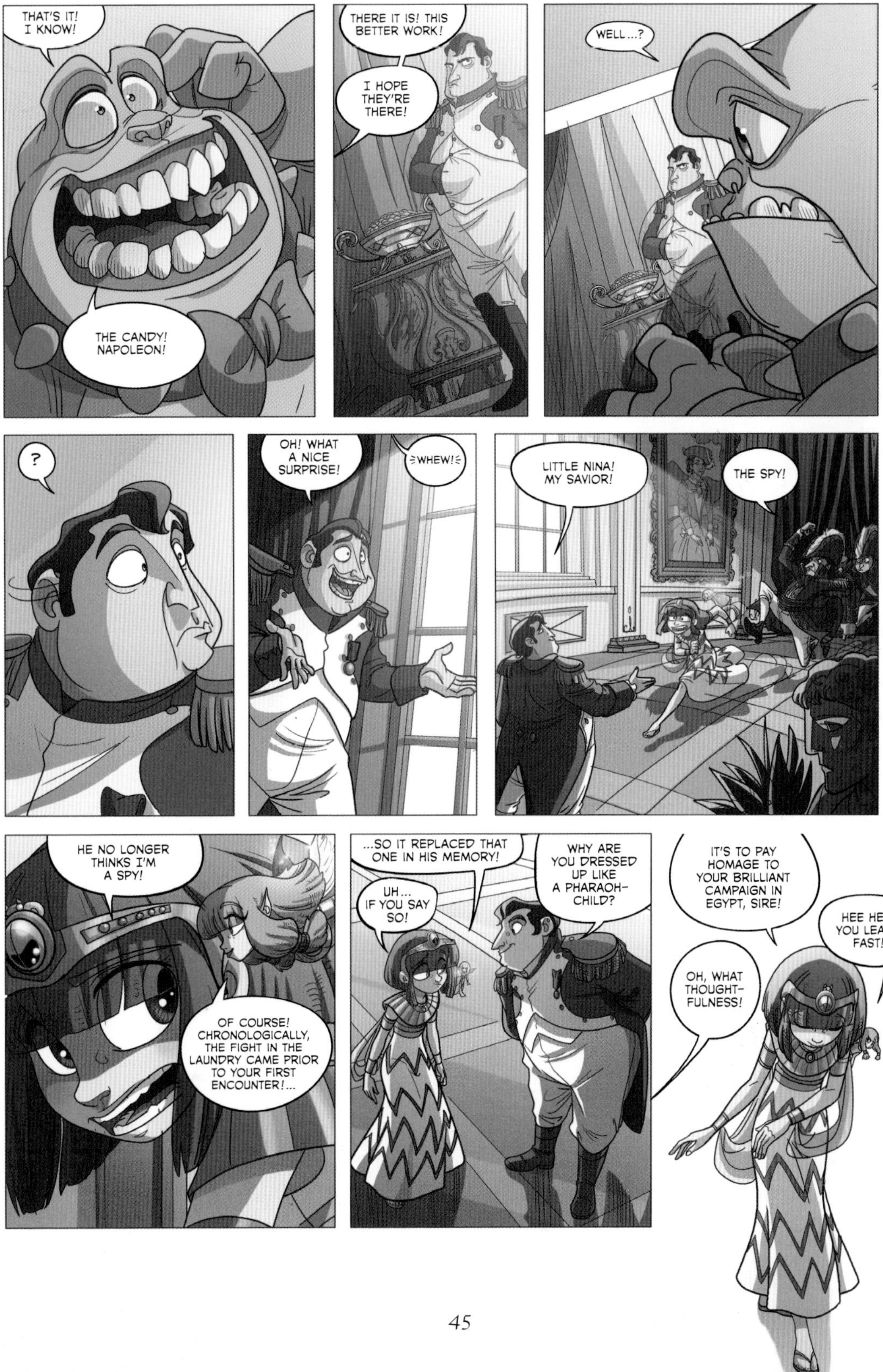
THAT'S IT! I KNOW!
THE CANDY! NAPOLEON!
THERE IT IS! THIS BETTER WORK!
I HOPE THEY'RE THERE!
WELL...?
?
OH! WHAT A NICE SURPRISE!
WHEW!
LITTLE NINA! MY SAVIOR!
THE SPY!
HE NO LONGER THINKS I'M A SPY!
OF COURSE! CHRONOLOGICALLY, THE FIGHT IN THE LAUNDRY CAME PRIOR TO YOUR FIRST ENCOUNTER!...
...SO IT REPLACED THAT ONE IN HIS MEMORY!
UH... IF YOU SAY SO!
WHY ARE YOU DRESSED UP LIKE A PHARAOH-CHILD?
IT'S TO PAY HOMAGE TO YOUR BRILLIANT CAMPAIGN IN EGYPT, SIRE!
OH, WHAT THOUGHT-FULNESS!
HEE HEE! YOU LEARN FAST!

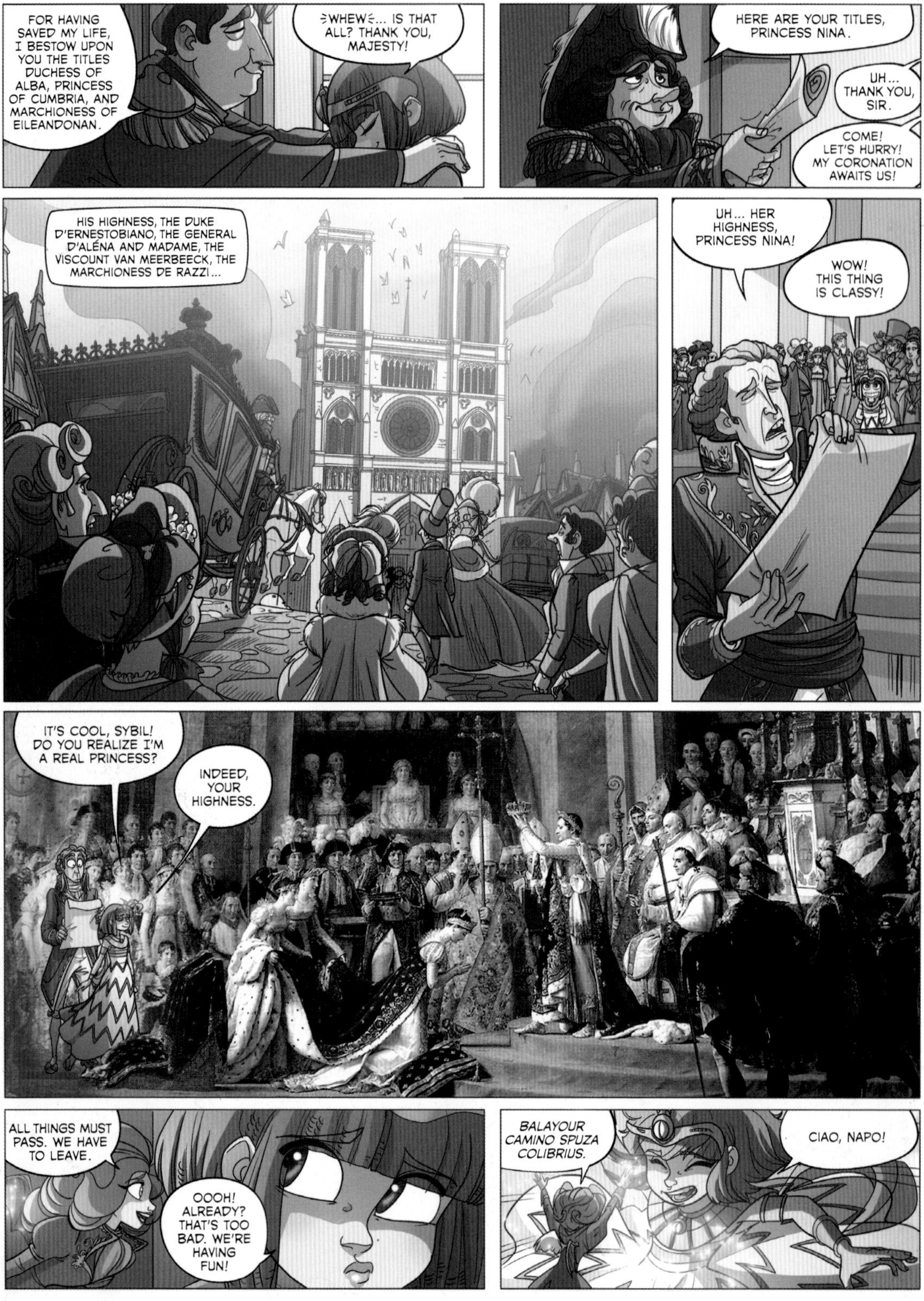
FOR HAVING SAVED MY LIFE, I BESTOW UPON YOU THE TITLES DUCHESS OF ALBA, PRINCESS OF CUMBRIA, AND MARCHIONESS OF EILEANDONAN.
WHEW... IS THAT ALL? THANK YOU, MAJESTY!
HERE ARE YOUR TITLES, PRINCESS NINA.
UH... THANK YOU, SIR.
COME! LET'S HURRY! MY CORONATION AWAITS US!
HIS HIGHNESS, THE DUKE D'ERNESTOBIANO, THE GENERAL D'ALÉNA AND MADAME, THE VISCOUNT VAN MEERBEECK, THE MARCHIONESS DE RAZZI...
UH... HER HIGHNESS, PRINCESS NINA!
WOW! THIS THING IS CLASSY!
IT'S COOL, SYBIL! DO YOU REALIZE I'M A REAL PRINCESS?
INDEED, YOUR HIGHNESS.
ALL THINGS MUST PASS. WE HAVE TO LEAVE.
OOOH! ALREADY? THAT'S TOO BAD. WE'RE HAVING FUN!
BALAYOUR CAMINO SPUZA COLIBRIUS.
CIAO, NAPO!

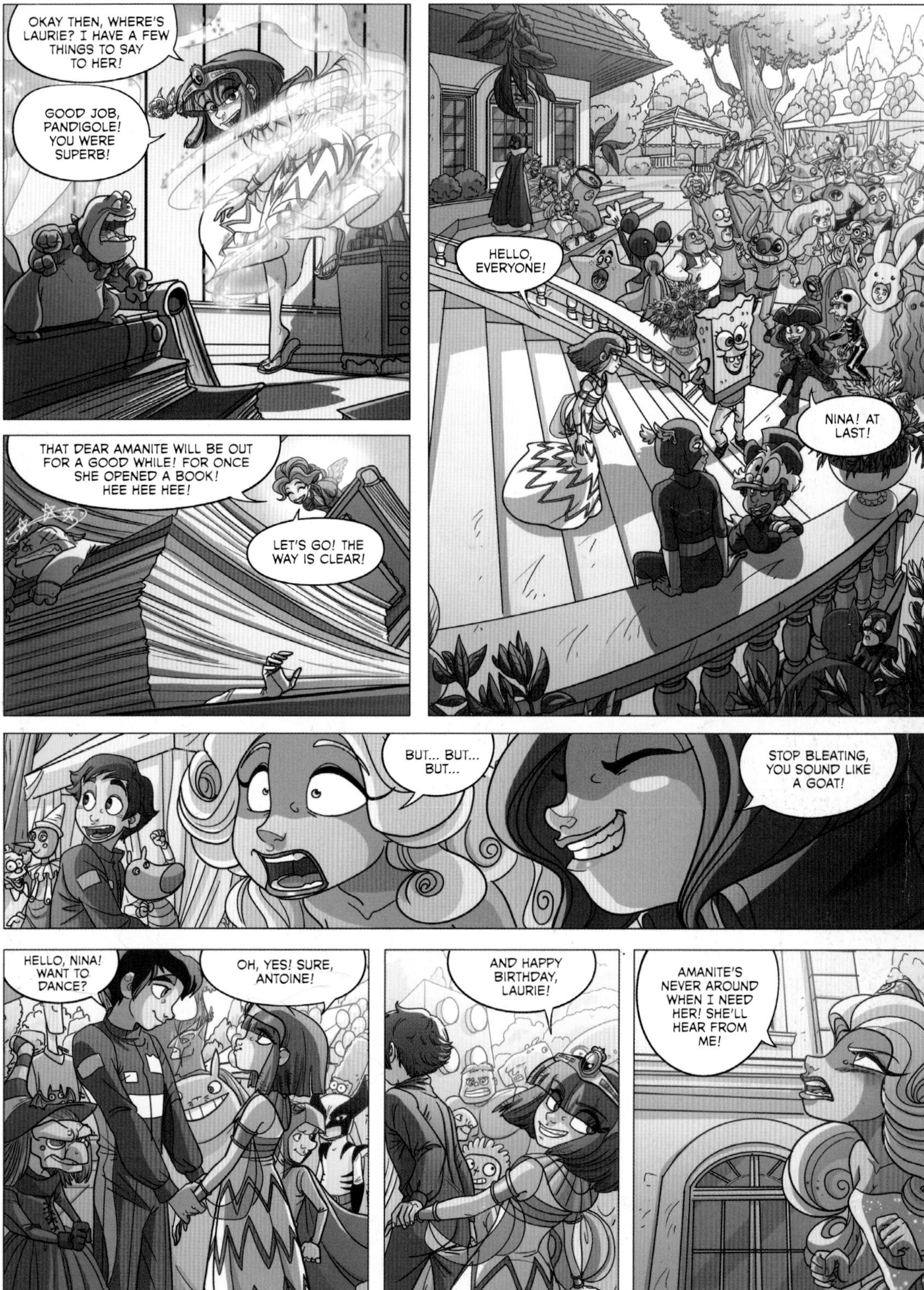
OKAY THEN, WHERE'S LAURIE? I HAVE A FEW THINGS TO SAY TO HER!
GOOD JOB, PANDIGOLE! YOU WERE SUPERB!
HELLO, EVERYONE!
NINA! AT LAST!
THAT DEAR AMANITE WILL BE OUT FOR A GOOD WHILE! FOR ONCE SHE OPENED A BOOK! HEE HEE HEE!
LET'S GO! THE WAY IS CLEAR!
BUT... BUT... BUT...
STOP BLEATING, YOU SOUND LIKE A GOAT!
HELLO, NINA! WANT TO DANCE?
OH, YES! SURE, ANTOINE!
AND HAPPY BIRTHDAY, LAURIE!
AMANITE'S NEVER AROUND WHEN I NEED HER! SHE'LL HEAR FROM ME!

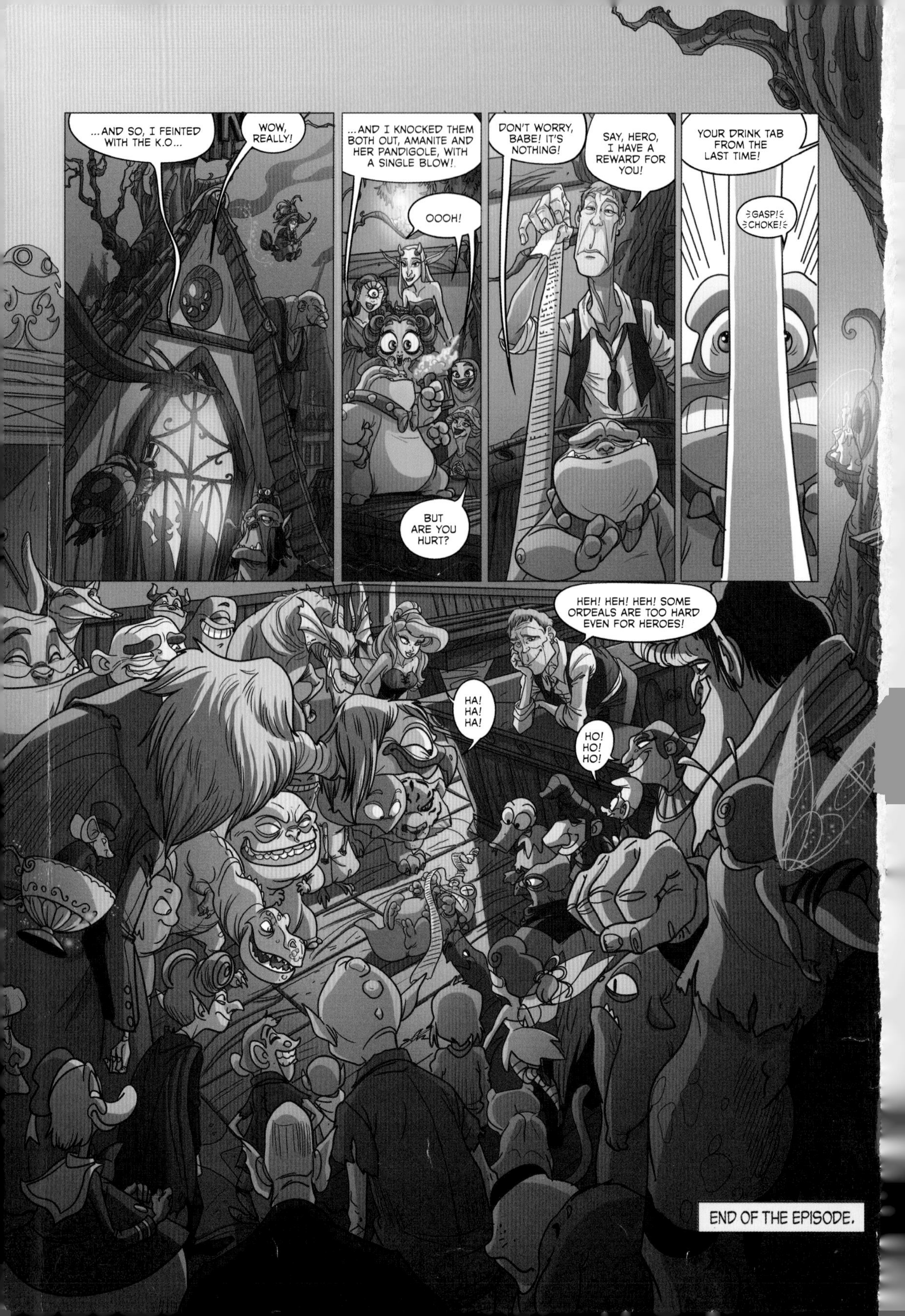
...AND SO, I FEINTED WITH THE K.O...
WOW, REALLY!
...AND I KNOCKED THEM BOTH OUT, AMANITE AND HER PANDIGOLE, WITH A SINGLE BLOW!.
OOOH!
BUT ARE YOU HURT?
DON'T WORRY, BABE! IT'S NOTHING!
SAY, HERO, I HAVE A REWARD FOR YOU!
YOUR DRINK TAB FROM THE LAST TIME!
GASP! CHOKE!
HEH! HEH! HEH! SOME ORDEALS ARE TOO HARD EVEN FOR HEROES!
HA! HA! HA!
HO! HO! HO!
END OF THE EPISODE.